Hilarious
Tales for Kids
and
Grown Ups

by

DEDWYDD JONES

Creative Fiction

For my dear daughters Caroline,
Awen and Caryl.

Again, with thanks to Maruti for invaluable
computer advice

"People of the world are so imbued with their own stupidity that they can never believe that one of their own has talent."
Marcel Proust to Mme Straus

"Be sober and hope to the end."
Peter 1.15

"Yer gotta larrf..."
Cockney private (Middx. Reg.) during the 3rd Battle of the Somme, July 12th 1916

CONTENTS

a fifteen-minute play
(Performed at The Royal Court Theatre, London, July, 2013. Director: Vicky Featherstone)

Hermione's Birthday Bubble

Hermione had just had her birthday party and the last of her tedious friends had left. Hermione was sick and tired of all the games and she sat sullenly on the sofa with her gifts around her. Why did Mum always give her the usual soft toys she was supposed to caress lovingly like some empty-headed cretin, while in reality, all she felt was a sense of rejection of the boring, glassy-eyed lumps of phony fur presented to her with such ecstatic cooings. 'Why do they treat us as if we're all infantile unthinking dunces, blind as bats?' - she asked herself for the umpteenth time. She struggled to acknowledge her Mum's half-hearted party gestures because she knew Mum made them just so her 'little Hermione' would feel guilty about rejecting them, if she ever dared to be so minded. "Hah!" she said out loud. "I know the tricks and motivations of these so-called grown ups. They are as an open book to me!"

She gazed with dislike at her presents, the Panda with its black and white coat and the fixed stare in its button eyes; the Clown, long out of his age group, with his usual phony, sickening wide cheesy grin; that bundle of silly feathers, the so-called 'Wise Gray Owl.' 'Where Gray Owl goes, Hermione is sure to go," her Mum had trilled to the guests, out of tune as usual. 'Not on your nelly!' thought Hermione, 'I will go where I alone want to go, bugger all wise owls!!' She sighed again. 'Why do grown ups treat me as if I have no real awareness of the world and the human beings around me? That stupid Panda! She threw it across the room, an eye bounced out. "Serves you right," she hissed at the offending beast. And that monkey with the fake red nose. That was supposed to make her laugh? She kicked him in the jaw and his false teeth flew

7

out. And then the Wise Gray Owl – Well, wee on, Gray Owl, he hadn't said a word since his first unwelcome appearance, the superior ponce. Who did he think he was kidding? Mary chucked him onto the floor. "Be wise over that," she said grinding her heel into his face. The Owl was supposed to be a sort of replacement father figure, she supposed, but her father never even bothered to come home let alone to her birthday parties and she couldn't blame him for that. She knew he drank on all occasions and slurred his words so badly he could hardly spit when he was too far gone. 'Know the psychological motivations of mankind," her Dad had once advised her with a cane , "and you won't get far. No one does. You'll fail. And people hate failures. They will then leave you alone!"

'Like father like daughter,' she nodded. Dad was OK, he rarely talked to anyone on two legs. He was good as his word. He talked to trees.

Thank God those childish hide and seek games were over, she sighed again, they usually ended in tears and slaps and howls and little treasures vomiting into the toilet bowl or failing to reach it and retching right down the line. That had been the case today too. With tears of fatigue and exasperation, her Mum had finally ushered her 'little guests' out of the house, muttering, "thank god that's over."

Hermione picked up one of the few satisfactorily pointless presents on the sofa, a big plastic bubble container, with a circular stick inside to wave the muck about. She shook it and from time to time made a few bubbles in the air. Some just hung there, like transparent snot off a nose. Others floated away. Small shit. Big deal. Huh! She gazed at the most repugnant gift of all - a huge doll, the Queen of the Fair Folk writ on her pale brow, with a deadly plastic crown, a false silk dress which twinkled with imitation diamonds and a silly magic wand in her hand, a bright foetid star on the end. That was Mum's gift! She always seemed to know just what Hermione detested! She leaned back sleepily, her gaze still on the ghastly Queen. Hermione's lids began to droop. Suddenly, she sat upright! What was this? Had the Queen's hand moved, just an inch? Yes! The Queen's eyes snapped open! A fixed expression of doll-like saccharine wonder at the world spread over her pink, painted face, but the rest of her remained immobile. Hermione spread a few bubbles in the air and decided to prod the static babe into a little action. She reached out with her plastic prodder and poked one of the small bubbles, hoping the explosion would wake up the Queen with a bump. But the bubble just bulged, as if impregnated, then expanding hugely until it was as big as a lift with a capacity of twelve. The Queen, now wide awake, beckoned to Hermione, "this way. Don't wee yourself, I know you've had enough." She guided Hermione up right inside the bubble. Hermione was too woozy to resist and went along quite passively, like a meandering bubble herself. She slumped down on the seats provided and gazed through half-closed eyes.

"You'll be lonely without your wicked friends, you'll miss them…" the Queen said in the soothing tones of a Swedish nanny. Hermione wondered for a second just who this creature had been talking to? "…so I'll fix that for you." She proceeded to prod her inert friends one by one, as at the receiving end of an electric goad, until they were herded into the bubble, Where they promptly sprawled on the seats, as lethargic and slack-jawed as any sloth on earth.

The Panda, the Monkey and the Clown sat right by the birthday gal. With a droop of the mouth, Gray Owl blinked nastily at her. 'With him by my side,' Hermione thought, 'I'll have little enough to laugh about for the livelong day.' Panda and Monkey, snapped at each other, and even aimed a scratch or two at their respective cheeks. Essentially, they were shivery, aloof, uncommunicative. The Queen gave them two fingers, party poopers, and stood at the steering wheel, the joystick. The bubble rose and floated around the room, somehow avoiding all the furniture. It went faster and faster in circles until Betsy felt an engine was bound to fall off. The Panda, Monkey and Clown oooh'd and aaah'd in a muted kind of way, but that was all. No one vomited. No one watched out for danger. The Queen turned the speed up to full until the bubble lurched, then bounded out of the open window into the huge gray day! As they moved along the cloudy firmament, Hermione gazed down at the suburban places, the empty chimney pots, the plots of tiny gardens, the ticky-tacky houses, and silly allotments. Hermione felt nothing but nausea for this way of life, essentially her own family's. A flock of Swans, their necks stretched out, whistled derisively at them as they passed. They all exchanged swear words, execrations and sarcastic laughs at each others' expense. The day and the company on both sides were all sneers and spittles. It was ghastly for everybody, which was fair enough, thought Hermione, given the nature of the unendurable human, his stinginess, his cruelty, his revolting idea of 'celebrations' and the bloodied earth itself.

They flew into black clouds of rain, but no riveting surprise event or any happenstance there. Hermione saw that she herself and her friends didn't get wet at all, not a drop fell on their indifferent half-baked bonces. They could see the storm on the outside, but the storm couldn't see them on the inside. The Queen dived to escape the typhoons, bugger the passengers, and the bubble obeyed her. Soon they were right down there shaken among the roof tops and gardens and conservatories of their decent neighbours and respectable friends. Hermione recognised, with compressed lips, her late guests and saw the little monsters, with the derisory adults, were showing their botties, mooning it was called, and making obscene gestures. 'The whole world had become one ugly grimace of ill manners and coarseness,' she thought. To complete the pretty picture, the Queen's passengers now joined in, revelling as much in the depths of grossness up in the air as much as at the bottom, on land. The Panda, the Clown, and the Monkey hawked up the last vestiges of phlegm from the party, and spat down onto their 'friends' who rushed indoors to escape the hostile, gobby, stinking showers. The monkey peed over them just that one time, to cheers and general approval. The Queen made sure Hermione received all the insults and calumnies meant for her in good part – I don't think! The fair pilot, she, the Queen, wasn't going to go gentle into that good night. She needed a fall-gal and Hermione was it!

But now it grew dark. Shadows lengthened as they do, over the trees, fields and domestic dwelling units. The enmity faded away into the blubbering twilight. The Queen slowed down, pulled open the curtains and went into a Stuka-dive-bomber swoop, then - plop! The big bang! The bubble burst - like life itself at the end of its lowest loop. The outraged beasties bumped down onto the sofa and began squabbling, with cries of revenge and threats of beheadings. The Queen silenced them with a single burp.

"Home again, huh, hell more like," muttered Hermione.

Hermione looked at the seething, resentful group. They didn't want to be there either. But who in the hell did?! Gray Owl reclined like a twat on the sofa with a bleary superior smile. He had had plenty of practice. Vanity and self-righteousness were his forte, the ruddy fink! Hermione sneered right back at him and gave two-fingers to the rest of them – dirty, late gate-crashers! They weren't supposed to be anywhere – the crud-heaps!

"What a disgusting way to end a birthday party," Hermione declared. The Queen just smiled and spat in noisy mendacious disagreement.

Hermione shook herself until she stood there right on the sofa, totally awake in the middle of her wretched birthday gifts and her happy home. She rubbed her eyes thoroughly again, and knew with a final sigh of relief it had all been a terrible nightmare, or had it? And did she care like a bat out of hell about it? No. An icy hand gripped her heart. She suspected these ghastly rides were far from over, far too many bubbles and grown ups to go. 'What a lousy conundrum for one so young,' she thought. 'Life is not fair. There is no god! There is no Paradise – just birthdays!'

How 'Q-Q' Taught Eleanor to Swim

Eleanor lived on a farm situated right out in the colourless countryside of Denge, East Anglia, the Fens, or something. The first thing you noticed about her home was that the farmyard was basically unkempt. Rusted harrows grew in the long grass, the odd plough lay half-submerged in the muddy ditch by the wrecked front gate; the hen coop had collapsed in ruins; the odour of dung hung in the air, unswept for weeks. The horses, cattle, pigs and sheep wondered about without let or hindrance, leaving their stinky visiting cards in byre, barn and front garden. The geese were particularly raucous and vicious, attacking anyone in sight, especially small children; the chickens pecked at everybody; the cocks woke everyone far too early, out of spite, of course; the pigs rooted the orchard and devoured the windfalls; the bog pond outside the gate, on the left, was full of common reeds, duck weed and a thin slick of ghastly greenish algae on hot summer days; the cows, god bless them, always hunkered down when they heard the cowman, Eleanor's Dad, coming ; the horses were released at dawn through the yard gate to disappear over the gray horizon, happy escapees; they wouldn't get in the way, as well, of Eleanor's Mum and Dad as they enjoyed doing just about sod all.

Eleanor possessed a natural dislike for animals. She invariably found them loathsome, with their filthy habits and foul odours. 'Quack-Quack,' the boy Drake, also known as 'Q-Q', was the least repulsive; but, nevertheless, just a low-down unexceptional drake, not a noble mallard, or a sweeping swan, a common or garden, flat-footed bloody barnyard water-fowl with a coarse, ear-busting voice, especially when aroused, with, seemingly, no other outstanding qualities of any kind, whatsoever, what a hero for a friend! Q-Q was said to be 'friendly.' Eleanor had seen little evidence of this but lived in the hope it would never happen. She didn't particularly like being with him, she just liked pushing him around and pretending to make him feel special, just like the bloody grown-ups and their families did in the district and indeed beyond, even unto into the outer parts of the world. Why Eleanor had any time for this scarlet-topped nonentity, no one was quite sure. Everyone jeered, but behind their hands (they didn't want to be seen as bad neighbours) when they saw the ignoramus Q-Q waddling after skinny Eleanor to share a bath in the brackish standing pond - whatever her Mum said, they hooted sotto voce between themselves. Eleanor was Q-Q's favourite grown up, and again everyone asked, why? Eleanor was tall, lanky, thin as a bean-pole, with straggly hair, glasses on her nose and braces on her teeth. She came 20th out of 24 in her class at school, no higher and no lower for years, a real stuck in the mud, a perfect mediocrity, fitting in well with the general character of the farm. In effect, Eleanor was as undistinguished as Q-Q. Perhaps that was this fatal attraction that did it, nonentity appeals to nonentity after all.

Eleanor scraped away the dried weeds from the mud on the edge of the pond and sat down, waiting for Q-Q to join her. She liked to keep Q-Q waiting. Q-Q knew this, and kept her waiting in turn, again just like the detestable grown ups, and this game could often go on for hours. Q-Q finally tottered up to her as silent as a fox and leapt into her lap. She pushed promptly him off and kicked him into the pond. "Not going to wash you today, your feathers are all congealed. Look, see the muck. And pigeon droppings on your head and stuff like that. Have a quick wash down, but all by yourself, it's essential, and be quick about it!."

Q-Q immediately leapt into the scummy waters. Eleanor was

right. For the last month, Q-Q had forgotten to take a bath and did not blame her for her harsh words and, besides, it was thrilling to get pushed around by the girl bean-pole, Eleanor. Her gaugings and thumps made him shudder with pleasure. After his five second tumble in the water, which the water lost, for it was muddier after he came out than before he went in, he emerged shaking off the bits of dislodged body gunge and settled down next to his Princess. She tested his wing feathers for damp. Q-Q at once objected, 'quaaack-quaaack,' he hated Eleanor disturbing his proud immaculate feathers, especially after a health-giving dip at her behest. Wasn't he her best comrade, after all, out of the whole lot of them?

But today, Eleanor found she had to keep a promise she had incautiously made to Q-Q the previous day – she had said that when Farmer Smith, Eleanor's Dad, was at Market, which he was to-day, she would take Q-Q for a ride in the 'new' boat which her Dad had built for her. She rued the day of the promise. Again, she was not sure why she had made it in the first place. 'What a drivelling idiot of a world it is sometimes,' she thought. Q-Q, she was convinced, was the worst possible passenger she could have chosen. He was a back-seat flyer. She had seen him badgering his fellow ducks in flight, and the thought never gave her a moment's peace. 'Do this, do that! all that manly ordure, up in the sky! What was it going to be like one earth, or water, same thing really.

And it wasn't really a boat at all. It was an old wash-tub thrown out with Queen Victoria into the mediaeval midden behind the rubbish tip, just rusting away with nowhere to go. Dad's best excuse for binning anything was his daughter, 'throw this out! Down the toilet with that!' etc. etc. so this article went, with his usual pretence of generosity, to lucky Eleanor! And it really was just a clapped-out wash-tub with a sail and a mast sticking up in the middle and a cross-seat from side to side, which creaked dangerously when sat upon, like sitting on the knee of the disintegrating human. Eleanor had been warned never to use it unless her Dad was there in a supervisory capacity, but today he was at the market, as previsaged by Eleanor- so now she came that deadly morning, she had to give her daily pest, Q-Q, his thrilling promised treat. Q-Q joined her on the brink. Hell, she pointed at the golden water-liliy which had come out overnight and was now, unforgivably, basking in the sun, like some typical fat bastard of a male. She would soon fix that! She dragged the intrepid tub out of the reeds, pushed Q- out of the way, jumped in, just, and began rowing ahead with the single oar. Q-Q was not in the least alarmed. He knew it was dangerous for Eleanor to try and sail the boat all by herself. Her Dad would give her an eyeful, sailing without his presence or permission! Q-Q cheered her on, daring her to go into still deeper waters. He jumped in and followed her. A puff of wind caught the sails and in a second, Eleanor found herself out in the middle of the pond. She tried to turn back but the wind was too strong. Q-Q leisurely followed her, swam around and around the boat, quacking in delight at her plight. He could see a rusty hole in the side of the old tub and that water was pouring in. He nearly applauded. Eleanor had got everything wrong, so right! She was in for a shellacking whatever the outcome. Eleanor jumped up in alarm, wailing and wringing her hands when she saw the boat was beginning to fill. Q-Q made triumphant, scoffing, quack-quacking noises, but after a few minutes, had tried to attract the other animals' attention. They must not miss the chance of revelling in the discomfiture of the bean pole, daughter of the wretched bosses of the world. First the water was up to Betsy's ankles, how she yelled! How Q-Q cheered her on! Then up to her knees - how she shrieked again! Perhaps she'd even drown, caloo callay! But Q-Q at last slowly stopped punching the air! All the animals who had joined in the mocking plaudits, making rude gestures from the safety of the bank, now also began having second thoughts. There was no doubt of it, the stupid tub was sinking fast, and Eleanor, the Princess of the Barn Yard, heiress of the whole hideous lot, was in it.

Q-Q now had to save his reputation. He embarked on a life saving demonstration, flapping his wings in the water, making motions like a swimmer doing the breast stroke, pretending to be drowning, laughing encouragement the while. Eleanor wriggled like a cornered tadpole and screamed back all the louder at the aquatic loon on her day of doom. But she was not the boss's daughter for nothing. She'd take the wind out of their sails! As the water reached her waist, she carefully studied Q-Q's motions in the water. He was not sinking, he was keeping himself alive, above water, by all these mad thrashings, and at the same time, still continuing to encourage her. She pushed herself into the water, stretched out her arms and swept them back, exactly as Q-Q was doing. She felt herself moving away in the water, yes, and now going forward, alright! faster and faster. She was swimming indeed! She closed her mouth in an ominous silence. Q-Q stopped his mockeries. This was serious. Damn, Eleanor was surviving. Eleanor kicked out and soon felt the ground under her feet. She crawled out breathless. She looked back and saw the mast of the sunken boat sticking up in the air. 'I did that,' she thought, 'to Dad's hideous old washing boat, thank god! What will he say? Who cares? I now know how to swim and it wasn't my fault!' She made faces at the now muttering, shamefaced, worried animals. To reveal the true state of her contempt, Eleanor now bent down, threw up her skirts to expose her skinny bum to them, the self same bare buttocks bum that had driven them into silence and surrender. She gave two fingers to the apologetic, stuttering Q-Q and poked out her tongue at him for good measure. Q-Q's hurrahs had died down once and for all, they were now as ashes in his mouth. Eleanor directed a last big juicy gob at the ruffled, humbled, mere man-drake! It covered his proud head feathers! She had made a complete fool of the noisy jumped up twat! He had shown her how to swim without even thinking he she was clever enough to develop such an essential skill so rapidly. He was the gutless thicko. She had been the born heroine and survivor all along. How Farmer Smith would deal with Q-Q, she could not say, especially if he was in a vinous rage! Bean Pole Eleanor now stood tall in the saddle and had proved herself indeed to be a true Princess-of-the-Farm-Yard-However-Neglected, and Q-Q would get all the blame for the entire sunken wreck, the shitty state of the premises, the grotesque untriumphal procession of the inhuman delinquent beasties, she would see to that. Q-Q would get it in the neck for it, and more than anything else, for teaching a mere girl female junior miss bean-pole, something useful. Yes, she thought gazing at the downcast, mumbling, animals at her feet, it was proving to be a very nasty day indeed for all of the others – but not for herself! She was still Daddy's least favourite daughter but she was one now who could swim on her own feet, float on her own back, and jeer in turn at the worst of the human sods in her life, on shore or on high, just like them. Let Dad put that in his grown up male paternalistic pipe and smoke it! She booted Q-Q out of the way and found herself well pleased with her victory and Q-Q's pathetic quacking along the way. No one challenged Eleanor after that ending!

Constanza's Treasure Hunt

Constanza was not enjoying herself at her birthday party. Her Mum had gone ahead with it against her wishes simply because she wanted to show off to the neighbours what a prosperous, kindly and generous parent she was. Her partner had excused himself on grounds of divorce, which had also put her in an especially bad mood. Angela, from next door, was Constanza's worst enemy, and her Mum's, the perpetual antagonist, always sniping at her from the rhododendrons to which Mum would reply with loud fart noises. The kids were already fed up, having been impressed into the party by their aggressive, unfeeling so called mature progenitors. The 'no-necks' ran around like sullen demented imps. How they yelled, trying for still more strident purposeless shrieks, for this was a meaningless, grown up treasure hunt, with nothing to relish in it, not even the jelly and custard, which was used mainly as artillery projectiles at all and sundry. As for the presents, they were the scrapings from the toy department of the yellow bins of the Co-op and Tesco's. These 'treasures' were invariably greeted with cries of derision and then crushed underfoot. Constanza's Mum had hidden all sorts of these tawdry gee-gaws inside the house and in the garden too, and pretended to be delighted each time one of her treasures was pounced on and worried to death. These elusive bits of tat were concealed inside boots and slippers by the back door, in saucepans and kettles in the kitchen, and even outside, it was such a lovely day to mess up, in buckets and watering cans, under rhubarb leaves and among gooseberry and blackcurrant bushes, there were even presents hanging up in the apple boughs like corpses in a country Western by the Cohen brothers, in next door's pear and cherry trees.

19

Constanza heard one of her fellow inmates screeching, "I've found a bloody Teddy!" That Teddy did not last five seconds. Another cried, "I've found a whole tea set!" that was smashed into fragments on the spot. Constanza looked on at the fun birthday rampage with equanimity, 'Going fine!' she said to herself, 'but I'd better hurry up or the presents will be all gone before I've had a chance to destroy them, such as they are.'

Then someone's little pest shouted gleefully, "Look what I've found!" And the ill-formed , boastful snotty called Angie held up a silk purse which jingled when shaken - money! Squeals of envy went up. A dozen grubby hands tried to snatch it but the possessor fought like a mongoose at its most vicious, clasped her treasure unyieldingly to her bosom and bore it away. Damn, thought Constanza, the only present worth anything, although Mum had only put the smaller denominations inside. As for the Lady of the House, she was certain she had done right to appeal to the inherent covetousness of her little charges. She had seen it throughout her life, especially among her jumped up, two-faced neighbours who'd skin a flea for a penny while pretending to insert a coin in the box for 'Save the Children'. Typical! Mum was pleased beyond expectation to see the greed and violence her little gift had inspired. Greed was the spur, she thought, not fame. Ask any adult - the mainspring of human emotion is cupidity!

Everyone began searching frantically again, and soon, almost everyone had found some sort of rag and bone reject or plastic discard. There was just one exception, the main reason for the party itself, pretty, strife-minded, spiteful little Constanza, who viewed her empty hands with dismay. "Oh," she thought, "what a cheap farce. I will not be humiliated. All these little pirana-fish from the area. I've got to turn up something. If not, I shall have to steal it.'

Then Constanza's Mum stood up by the back door and clapped her hands like a Headmistress with her strident clanging bell, and shrieked. "Listen! Listen everybody! Now," she yelled again, "there's only one present left and I can tell you it's a pretty special one. Look for an envelope with a red ribbon. Try to find it now, before tea-time."

Every beastly little guest scurried off in all directions, their avarice aroused anew, with theft as their guide, and slaughter and destruction as their banner in the van.

'Wouldn't every little corporal love to be dictator, even if just for a day!' Constanza knew that. She could hardly believe that her Mum and Dad, grown ups to a man, had remained for so long in such ignorance.

Constanza searched and searched till it seemed there were no places left to look. But the last special present had to be there somewhere, her ghastly Mum had said so and she would undoubtedly have planned for a last unrestrained riot of grabbit-and-run, so her guests would go homeward howling with bloody noses, hostilities thankfully re-established for at least two months.

Constanza wondered off to the bottom of the garden. She peeped at the empty flower borders next door. No U boats on the starboard bow! Leaning against a pear-tree was a rickety ladder and it led right up into the middle of the branches. 'Perhaps that's where the last present is,' Constanza thought, 'trust Mum.'

If nothing else, Constanza would have loved to add a little more enmity to the celebrations, the cherry on the hate cake,' she christened it. She wriggled through the hedge, and began climbing the ladder. She got more nervous the higher she climbed. Then she heard her friends cheering in savage triumph, each yell followed by crashing sounds and fiendish laughter. What triumphant hullabaloo! Had they found it, the last gift. Constanza imagined tearing the legs off the little tykes like some repulsive spider from the wainscoting. She climbed even faster.

Suddenly, from just above her head came a wild ,"Caw, caw!" and a big glossy black jackdaw swooped down from its nest and flew around her head, flapping its wings aggresively. Penny trembled. She had heard that jackdaws always went for the eyes. She clung on to the ladder and tried to shoo the angry predator away. It finally flew off with more loud, evil "Caw, caws!" with a look in its eye which said, "I'll be back!" She breathed a sigh of relief. She had to get out of this. Angela's pseudo-posh Mum was bad enough, but the jackdaw was worse. It was the eyes. She was about to climb down when she saw something sparkle through the leaves. There! It flashed again. Was this the last present? she thought. She pushed the branches apart and there in the crook of the branches lay the jackdaw's nest. Something was shimmering and glimmering inside. She reached in and felt around with her fingers. Slowly she pulled out a string of pearls, then a ring of pure genuine shining gold. Surely her Mum knew of this treasure trove. Had she left them there just to test her honesty? You could never tell with dear Mum. You always had to proceed with caution with all matters relating to finance. Holding her precious finds tight, Constanza climbed down, wriggled back through the hedge and ran up the garden to the house, where her Mum and her snappy, disgruntled guests were gathered. Mum was braying again for all the neighbours to hear, as well as the snotties, "And the last present is…!" She held up an envelope tied with a red ribbon and slowly opened it. "Here it is, the last treasure!" She held it aloft again, so no one could miss envying it, "a free ticket to the best seat in the circus which has just come to town. And it goes to our dearest neighbour, Angela!" As Angela reached out greedily for the ticket, there were suppressed groans, glowerings and stampings of feet. Mum gave Angela the last of the most perfunctory and meaningless kiss of the afternoon. Mum loved the day, it had been a triumph of the posh over the arrivistes, like Angela and her coarse tribe, whatever the quality of the presents.

"And worth a penny or two too," thought Constanza, looking at the envelope, 'clever Mum, perfect timing to make them full of grasping tendencies and feelings of robbery with violence, before they go home. Typical,' but Constanza was already planning how to turn the situation to her advantage.

"No! Stop everyone. Look!" she shouted, "look at what I've found!"

She held up the string of pearls, then the gold ring. Judy's Mum stood still, dumbstruck. She reached out hardly believing her eyes, and felt the pearls between her fingers. "Just imitation," she finally declared, tossing them aside, looking at Penny disdainfully, "not worth a sou. How could you have been so taken in, girl?" But she fell silent when Penny held up the ring. "But... but...my ring, my dear mother's wedding ring!" Mum paused, then inspected it closely, slipped it on and off her finger. It fitted perfectly. 'Stolen, no doubt,' she thought to herself, glaring in the direction of Angela's house. But she looked again. The inscription inside showed it was the actual genuine ex-possession of her departed Mum. She held it up it and shouted, "This ring, this band of gold of my mother, is back home and it is mine, all mine!" Uneasy silence greeted this announcement. She thrust the ring into the pockets of her tight jeans. No one was going to get it out of in there! And looking at the upturned, hostile faces, she decided to hang on to the last ticket. That red-ribbon envelope was not going to a nest of vipers, a mere den of nouveau riche pillagers. At that moment, a shadow flitted over them all, and down swooped the jackdaw, cawing angrily. 'you bloody human robbers!" it seemed to be shrieking at them, 'Greed! Greed!! GREED!!!! Caw! Caw!! Caw!!!"

Mum promptly yelled back, "you'll never see this ring again, you black streak of piss, no thanks to you or to anyone here or in that garden of Angela's, the poor light-fingered cow next door, it is back in its rightful home. Remember only this, from now you are dealing only with me, Constanza's Mum, the doyen of the district, the slap in the face of every man!" The Jackdaw flew off really put off by the cutting timbre of Mum's voice, cawing and flapping its wings in rage and frustration.

"Constanza," said Mum, "as for you - a special present. Two free tickets to the Zoo, one for you and one for your wonderful friend Angela! Angie, from next door.' Her toady 'no-neck' audience almost cheered. Were they to be so favoured next?! Not on their nelly, mate. Constanza looked on at her Mum, almost with admiration. Mum had done it again, she had failed the winner, won the loser, overcome the neighbours, recovered a valuable ring, sent the jackdaw pecking, dominated the proceedings! Queen of the shit-pile! Great stuff!

She shook a finger at Constanza, "And don't you ever go climbing trees again next door, it'll get us a bad reputation." She paused, "won't it?" she demanded of her now subdued, shuffling guests. They mumbled their hang-dog agreements like sheep on the edge of a cliff. 'Well done, Mum,' thought Constanza, 'Neat. All these little sods meek as spit, in the palm of your hands.' And then, whammo, bammo, dammo! - Constanza got it - she now too confronted the crowd of invitees, and beamed, simply beamed. She beamed like her mother, she beamed like her grandmother, she beamed at everyone, even a fart in the hedge would have got one! -

yes, at last, in an instant, she was beaming at all her best friends, the most wonderful neighbours in the world, each one, and so she said out loud so next doors for miles could hear, "Bye bye, my lovely dear little guests! Don't Mum and I have the good fortune to have the best friends and best family in the world?!" and, on top of her beamings into outer space, she blew loads of kisses at them. And they responded in the same brotherly, sisterly, motherly, neighbourly manner, all shining teeth, auld lang synes, all clappings, and kiss-throwings like everyone else was doing all the time to each other. Never totally meaningless, of course; never utterly false, just absolutely typical, for the crow is never far away, nor the red-ticket of avarice. Yes, thought Constanza, 'there is no purgatory, there is no limbo, there are no seven circles of hell, there's just mummies come to their term!' And after the stunning success of this one, Constanza and her Mum had surely become the leading hostesses of the executive homes of the district, if not county.

'Bloody Constanza,' thought Mum, looking at her clever daughter with new eyes, 'not bad, bitch. That was almost grown up.'

How Hathaway learned to Sing

Hathaway was sitting under the cherry tree in the garden. It was April and the tree was covered with big, pinkish-white, fluffy blossoms. It was sunny and the birds were trilling and whistling. The songs were coming from all directions - 'I'll Walk the Line,' 'Rocket Man,' – Hathaway noticed they were really golden oldies this particular morning, from another epoch, tunes sometimes favoured by her conservative Mum, even, shockingly, 'Mother's little Helper,' 'Not Fade Away,' by the rebellious, hairy rolling groans, and then, in an agony of yearning, Alexander heard her favourite, 'I had a Dream,' by the true immortals, Abba. The melody raised her up on invisible wings and transported her to an entirely different plane of feeling, where longing was queen and nostalgia a way of life. Hathaway wept in unquenchable melancholy as she always did when she visited the Abba Yearningland. The song sobbed to a close, like Hathaway, and then again she felt the immemorial loneliness coming. But merry, moping, blackbird jargoning irresistibly arose in the bushes. Hathaway wished she could sit at the top of a cherry tree and chirrup all day. She closed her eyes and imagined she was up in the branches next to the sky, singing away. Abruptly, she heard a rush of wings and found a shiny blackbird perched next to her, watching with a very engaging look in his eyes. 'Blackbird he is, so 'Blackbird' shall be his name,' thought Hathaway. Blackbird cocked his head and fluttered his wings in a bow, and began singing. Hathaway sat up. Blackbird was singing her number one, 'I had a dream…' Hathaway was so caught up in the soaring Abba scales, she tried to join in. Blackbird slowly came to a halt.

"Please do not do, 'I had a Dream...' like that," he admonished her, "without a little practice."

"But blackbirds don't talk," gasped Hathaway, momentarily miffed by the sound of a blackbird's voice.

"Not only can we talk," replied Blackbird, "we can sing, and we can sing better than you!"

"I was doing my best," said Hathaway, a bit put out, she had always thought she had a little talent, however minor.

"Don't worry," said Blackbird in a kindly way, "we sing all day, you see, so we all know all the tunes of all the best songs."

"I was listening to you and your friends very attentively."

"It's nice to have a sympathetic audience."

"How do you manage to sing like that all the time? I mean you were going through the golden oldies as if it was yesterday."

"There is no yesterday for a good melody. Look where you landed with Abba. What day was it then?"

"It was, well, all the time, every day, sort of...I see what you mean! But how do you manage it?"

"I sing in the morning, I sing in bed, I sing in the bathroom, I sing in my head. That's how. Don't you ever do that?"

"I try," said Hathaway, "but it doesn't seem to help."

"'Scuse me," said Blackbird, and flew higher into the tree.

Hathaway could hardly see him for the blossoms and branches.

"Come up and sit by me," she heard him say.

"I'd love to," said Hathaway, "but which is the way up? I can't see you."

"Just follow my tune," he said and hummed snatches of 'I had a Dream,' as Hathaway climbed up and sat on his right hand side.

"I know girls don't usually climb trees," said Blackbird, "but if you want to sing, you've got to learn to climb up trees like this."

"I hardly felt I was climbing," said Hathaway, "more like sort of floating."

"That was the song," sang Blackbird.

Hathaway settled down happily. She was hidden in drooping leaves and spreading blossoms. No one below could see her, no one above could see her, the only person who could see her, was tuneful, golden-oldie Blackbird, sitting by her. Blackbird raised a wing.

"I know very well which tune first launched you into the blue beyond up in the clouds," he said and this time sang, "I had a dream..." all the way to the end. Sue listened open-mouthed. It was so beautiful, it was as if as Abba was right there singing along with Blackbird, but also there again with her all those years ago, in her dim, distant and aching ' childhood', was it? Her heart beat fast. Out of time. Abba had transported her again. They never seemed to fail! Suddenly, the cherry tree was full. Blackbirds were perched in rows, all with their heads on one side, as if enjoying the music of the new pupil. Blackbird raised its wing "Now," said Blackbird, "we'll sing slowly so you can follow us." Sue began singing, 'I had a Dream…' and every time she made a mistake, the blackbirds would stop and sing the right note until Hathaway could sing the whole of it straight through without a break. Again she floated upwards and upwards…until her eyes snapped open in surprise and found she was still sitting under the cherry tree. Had it all really happened? Just then her Mum shouted from the back door, "Time for tea!"

As Hathaway walked up the garden path, she began singing, 'I had a Dream…' and there was not one single mistake. Her Mum looked up as she entered the kitchen, "where on earth did you learn to sing like that?" she asked.

"I don't really know," stammered Hathaway.

"Well, go on, sing it again."

And Hathaway did, straight through. Later, when Hathaway won the prizes for the best singer in the school, her mother would say, "I don't know how Hathaway learned to sing like that, she sings just like a Blackbird!"

Miranda and the Sea-Shells

Miranda and her Mum were coming back from a gray, dreary day at the sea-side. Miranda was sitting by the window, disconsolate and downcast, but with a secret smile on her face, which her Mum hated. What was going on in the child's head? - watching the drizzling raindrops on the panes and grinning like an ape. The trees whizzed past, but not fast enough for Miranda. She wished this part of the miserable trip was over. Why didn't her Mum just leave her alone with her friends on her free days. And didn't her Mum always moan that all she wanted too was to be left alone too. And yet she insisted on these pointless trips which she didn't enjoy, the opposite in fact, judging by the sour look on her face. And yesterday when she had wanted to go to the pictures, her Mum had flatly refused even when Miranda pointed out in the programme – "look, only, 'moderate violence, only two uses of strong language, only one sex reference, and no injury detail!' Mum, that wouldn't corrupt a flea, you could show it in a Nunnery!"but her Mum remained obdurate, 'none of this filthy fare for my daughter!'

Why were grown-ups so two-faced? And why didn't they give the kids some allowance for their ten years, more or less, and talk straight. They could see better through their elders than the elders could see through them! 'Impenetrably short-sighted!' she thought. Her Mum closed her eyes and groaned softly. That stupid daughter! This ghastly weather! That stupid droop of Miranda's lips. What a day! 'What have I done to deserve this?' she asked herself and lapsed into an ineffectual doze.

"Soon be there," Miranda had said, nearly out loud to herself as they were arriving, she had to talk to somebody! - looking at the trees fast vanishing into the rainy haze, although she'd known that was no sort of consolation. She'd thought of the sea-shore books she had studied in preparation for this visit. 'What is the point,' she had thought, 'if you can't share it.'

'Talking to herself again,' her Mum had thought, 'as if I wasn't there.'

Miranda glanced at her mother, 'Still mumbling away,' she thought, 'they always do that.' She watched the scudding clouds with a far-away look in her eyes. Again she re-visited her little sea-side Nirvana, but on the quiet.

"Well, you are a silent one today, aren't you," said her Mum, surfacing to consciousness at last, determined to say something which would make Miranda uncomfortable. Miranda recognised the provocation but didn't take the bait. 'Here we go again,' she thought.

"You did enjoy the beach, I hope, it took ages to arrange the trip for you - didn't you?" urged Mum with a positive note of spite in her voice.

"Oh, yes, I really did!" said Miranda with such bouncing sarcasm, she was certain her Mum would notice. But, no, she was still too bound up in her own misery. Mum looked down with disapproval at the sea-shells Miranda was holding in her lap. There were cockle-shells and scallop and needle shells, sting winkles, beautiful blue periwinkles, and even a few violet sea-snails, and a magnificent iridescent conch shell which seemed to whisper with seas and lapping wavelets, even from a distance. They were all strung together onto a shiny silver thread. The shells clacked and glittered when Miranda moved.

31

"Oh, do stop that Miranda, such a noise."

Miranda stiffened to a full stop and made like a statue. Her Mum nodded, yes, that was the way it should be with the young uns, a perpetual marble silence. She promptly broke her own rule.

"You were lucky to find those shell things,' she said, "you don't get that kind of luck often, do you, do you?" Miranda remained mute. "It's an awful day, and you're just as bad, so ungrateful. And those shells smell. You don't know what I've sacrificed for you."

'Yes,' thought, Miranda, she could have been 'a star or win on 'Britain's got Talent Show,' something as ugly and pointless as that! Grown ups! They always say the same thing. Well, it's not my fault. When I make a mistake I admit it and try to do better, Mum just nags and tries to do worse. Who'd be a grown up? They were such unhappy beings, she thought, before lapsing into the simmering silence again. End of chat. Her Mum would not even begrudge her the arrows of outrageous fortune. What had they got to do with her? Well, things had gone better than her dreary old Mum would ever know. Miranda gave that secret little smile again. She wouldn't tell anyone except her friends at school, but never her Mum - she was too down-in-the mouth on a permanent basis, not even a bowl of cherries would cheer her up.

She recollected the extraordinary events of the day. She had been walking along the beach all by herself, collecting shells. Her Mum was fast asleep on a blanket on the sands higher up. After the big storm there were shells everywhere. They were in the pools on the rocks, on the tide-line and still more were being pushed in by the waves. Her bag was already half-full. She saw a line of shells leading round a great pile of fallen rocks. She turned the corner and paused in surprise. In front of her, loomed a dark cave. The trail of shells went straight into it. The shells here, she noticed, were particularly big and shiny. She decided she had to have some of them to show her friends at school. She followed the line right into the cave. The shells here were scattered around and they shone with all the colours of the rainbow. They were so bright she could see every inch of the way. She followed them until she came to a deep sandy pool. It was green and calm and the shells lead down right into the water. Miranda noticed a beautiful yellow and purple conch-shell by the side of the pool. She picked it up, she felt she could almost play on it, so redolent was it of the sea-shore, cries of gulls and the sound of rushing waves. She dropped the shell in surprise as a commanding little voice cried out from below,

"Oh, not again! Not that one!"

She peered down. A little figure emerged from the pool, shaking himself dry. She knew what he was from the sea-shore books at school, he was a little sea-manikin, a sometimes friendly denizen of the deep, no bigger than half a human child, a near relative of the Queen of the Fair Folk of Iffland on her vast estates. He had on a pointed green cap and wore a cloak of spreading sea-lettuce with gold threads in it. Round his neck, he had on a brilliant necklace of glowing sea-shells which rattled as he spoke. His face was sharp and pointed, but his eyes were friendly. He shook a finger at Miranda.

"I've been watching you!" he said, pointing at Mirandas's bag, "taking our best shells."

Miranda felt guilty, not only because he was angry but also because she knew he understood what she had done.

"I'm so sorry," she said, "I didn't I know they belonged to anyone."

"They belong to the folk of the sea, like me," he said, pointing to himself.

"But who are you?" Miranda asked.

"I'm a Sea-Manikin," he replied, "anyone can see that. Jerome by name."

"But I've never seen a Sea-Manikin before," said Miranda, especially a Jerome one."

"Well, in that case, how do you do?"

He bowed elegantly and shook Miranda's hand warmly.

"So sorry Jerome, you can have all the shells back. Here." She offered the bag.

"Listen, my dear Miranda, it is an honour to meet a human who understands us manikins so well and who possesses such a generous heart and who is not afraid to say sorry and offer immediate redress after committing an error. It's just you pick the best ones," he explained with an understanding smile.

"And nearly shattered my life!" shouted a gruff voice at her feet. She looked down. An ancient hermit crab was crawling out of the sand carrying his moveable home, a yellow giant winkle, on his back. He reared up and waved a claw at Miranda.

"Trying to dispossess me, trying to take the roof off my head, waking up an OAP crab as if it was his last day on earth!" he said accusingly.

"This is Phillip," Jerome at once tried to establish peace, a quality he loved, especially when shared with his neighbours.

"I never meant it, really," pleaded Miranda," I love hermit crabs and I've never eaten one in my life. I dropped you like a hot coal when I saw your claw. I put you back, I really did. Look, you're home again."

"She didn't do it on purpose," said Jerome, "and she has expressed genuine remorse."

"Really?"

"Truly!"

"Well, I forgive you then," said the Phillip, "I have to sleep a lot, you see." His eyelids drooped as if he was going to doze off on the spot. He shook himself and yawned again.

"Why," he said, "Miranda, you love shells almost as much as we. I tell you what," he said to Jerome, "let's show Miranda why we're so careful about keeping our best shells."

"I was just going to suggest that," said Manikin.

"Well, follow me then!" cried the Phillip and slipped without a splash into the pool and disappeared.

"Our turn," said Jerome, taking Miranda's hand.

"But how can I breathe down there?" she asked in alarm.

"Leave that to me," said Manikin. "Just follow me."

"I don't know," said Miranda, looking nervously into the pool.

"You don't know because you live in the town and only come to the beach once every summer. But we live in the middle of the sea and never leave it. So we **know**! Now you're going to see just what we manikins and crabs and folk persons of the oceans can do. Hold my hand tight, close your eyes and you'll be able to go wherever you wish, even **under** the sea!"

Miranda screwed up her courage, held on tight to Jerome's hand, and let herself slip into the water, just like Phillip. She sank down, down, and nearly shouted out in fear, but then her feet touched the bottom. She was safe. Then she felt herself moving, as if in an invisible bubble. She was dry, she could walk, she could speak. She stood there unafraid!

"Don't hold your breath," said Jerome.

"But I can breathe," she gasped.

"And talk, too," said Jerome with a laugh. "Now open your eyes."

Miranda's her eyes grew rounder and rounder as she looked. She found she was standing in the middle of what looked like a new toy town. The houses were hardly bigger than the toys at home. But the houses were made of sea-shells. The walls were built of sparkling periwinkles, the roofs of scallop-shells, the pathways of mother-of-pearl. Around every house were floating gardens of sea-weeds, bladder-wrack, kale and sea-lettuce, food for generations. The whole town shone with all the brightness of every colour she had ever known. The sea-manikins were everywhere but Miranda saw lots of the other folk too, the people of the sands – the cushion stars, sand hoppers, dog whelks, sea urchins and horses, the prickly sunstars, and they were all intensely busy. They stood around mounds of shells in front of the houses, building still more. As one house was completed, so another went up. Then she understood, it was all for one, and one for all. She was privileged to see the many musketeers, boys and girls, of the fraternal deep-sea scene. That's why, she realised, they were all smiling. She saw Phillip fixing a splendid yellow conch-shell onto his front door, his door-knocker! He waved cheerfully to Miranda and all the others turned and waved too, many blowing on their conches. What a wonderful symphonic welcome from truly happy neighbours, not as up there in the 'real' world, a vale of misery if there ever was one, she thought, but right down here is the place to be, where one little paddle-worm is worth more than a million fully grown adults any day up there!

"Now you can see why we were so worried," explained Jerome

"But why are they all waving at me so happily?"

"Well, our Phillip told them all how much you love sea-shells and that you were bringing them all back for their homes."

Miranda at once handed her full bag of shells to Phillip. He held them up in his claws, and all gave three cheers for Miranda. Jerome beckoned to his friends and they all gathered round.

"We don't mind you collecting shells," said Jerome, "but don't take the best ones, all at once, please."

"I promise I won't ever again!" said Miranda.

How civilized they were. No nagging, no threats, just an explanation and a happy invitation to understand and be a part of it, to share, to give and take, the last thing a grown up would ever do, especially the thick-eared, hard-hearted Mums and their diktats. They only thing they shared above, was their wretchedness, their authority fixations and greed.

"Then you shall have your reward," said Jerome and he took off the marvellous necklace he wore around his neck. He pulled a silver thread from his cloak, and all his fellow citizens came one by one and slipped a shining sea-shell onto the thread. Hermit crab gave her one of his wonderful yellow conch shells. Miranda gave him a big kiss. Phillip beamed with delight. Everyone clapped and blew kisses as Jerome put the necklace around Mirandas's neck.

"We all love shells here," said Jerome, "just like you. Shells are home. That's why you can wear these shells now, just like us and feel at home too."

Jerome suddenly cocked his head to one side and listened intently.

"Yes," he said, "time to go back now, Miranda, your Mum is getting antagonistic."

Sadly, Miranda looked round for the last time at her new friends

"Don't feel sad, Miranda," said Jerome, "but if you ever do, just hold your necklace and think how happy you've made us and you'll be happy too, at home. Now close your eyes and hold my hand tight."

Miranda hung onto Jerome's hand and felt herself rising up, as in a balloon. With a sudden bump, she found herself sitting on the edge of the pool in the cave. But it was dark now and all the shells had disappeared. She looked around for her musketeer, Jerome, but he had gone insubstantial too. Where were they? Then she remembered the necklace in her hand, and held it tight and at once she could see the cockle–shell town and the sea-happy folk. What Jerome had said was true. Every time she touched a shell, she felt at home, at ease, happy and free – well, a bit!

Then in the distance she heard he Mum yelling, "Miranda!

Miranda! Where are you!?" Miranda had no option. She ran out of the cave.

"Miranda," said her Mum, "where have you been? I was beginning to…" She was about to clout her daughter when her eyes fell on the necklace.

"Where did you get those?"

"Oh, just by a pool in the cave."

"They're …sort of… nice," she declared reluctantly,

Her Mum inspected each shell in turn, wondering if they were worth anything, "why," she finally exclaimed, "each one is worth… er… is prettier than the last! Takes all sorts, I suppose. Well, hurry up, we've got a train to catch and it's starting to rain again. Bloody typical!"

Later, when Mirands was watching the soggy trees as they whizzed by, her Mum frowned at her for the hundredth time.

"Why, Miranda, " she demanded, "why have you got that stupid grin on your face all the time? It's most irritating."

Miranda turned to stone, just as her Mum wanted, held on to the shells, immediately felt quite at home, and, of course, smiled again. Jerome and the Fair Folk of Iffland were still with her.

Bartholomew Bear and the Honey Pot

Bartholomew Bear was no baby but he woke up rubbing his tummy. He looked around his dismal bedroom, cautiously got out of bed, and tip-toed into the kitchen. He was ravenous. He hadn't eaten a thing for five months. What a thing to do to one so young, he thought, what were the grown ups thinking of? Yet he felt he understood their situation - just. But he wished they understood his, just a bit! It all echoed in his brain, 'Save up the calories for a snowy day, store the honey against famine!'

"But Mummy, listen to my stomach," he pleaded, "it's rumbling."

"No, it isn't, child!"

"Yes, it is!"

"Don't you dare contradict your Mum!" roared Daddy Bear, "that's my job!" and gave his baby son the usual clout across the snout which sent him sliding across the floor.

It was like this every night - curt orders and cuffs across the nose. Why did his Mum and Dad insist so implacably on this robust ceremony. Apart from the food imperatives, there were the 'bed' ones too, "Time for bed this instant!" "No, you can't have a drink of water!" "Go to sleep or it's curtains.' And the final shout, "Not a crumb! Five weeks to go, I want to hear you snoring this instant!" Mum would send him to Dad again who would clout him and send him back to Mum who would also clout him, till he got so tired of life, he fell fast asleep. But he was finally realizing the reason for all this physical and moral dominance, his parents were simply down and out bullies. Yes, he had to admit it. Didn't they do the same to all those in the immediate vicinity, the bunnies, the badgers, hares, weasles, voles and moles, always giving them orders, booting them out of his way, stealing their nuts and bits of stray fabric, their clothes, leaving their homes destitute of the creature comforts. And they all obediently gave him what he demanded. Wasn't Daddy Bear the hugest grizzly this side of the red woods, with claws as long as Wolverine's and just as destructive. By day, in public, the parents pretended to be, 'cuddly' 'wooly,' 'friendly,' and 'good neighbours.' OK, OK, but they had never got the message about Bartholomew, their only begotten son and heir, he was now old enough not to be cuffed around like a stupid mutt!

Bartholomew looked around the kitchen. What a mess. Mummy Bear had tried to make it cosy underfoot, admitted, but she had run out of sheeps' wool, goose feathers, skins and pelts, leaving many bare spaces, and there were draughty corners and windy cracks in every window pane. Daddy Bear had stacked up piles of straw in the bedrooms for their long sleep, but some of it had turned black in the rain before he had brought it in, and it had rotted quietly away, without redress. When Bartholomew objected to the smell, Daddy Bear just shrugged his mighty shoulders and told him, 'For goodness sake, stop moaning like your Mother, the straw is top notch, go to sleep!'

Next to the living room was the parents' bedroom and it was very comfy. Mum and Dad had sunk all their differences, for once, and had foraged for the best remnants they could find among their neighbours' possessions. They made sure they could sleep like logs and dream of Bear Heaven, without as much as a drop of a pin disturbing them. Their home lay inside an enormous hollow oak in the middle of the woods. Its many layers of fallen leaves and heavy branches helped to keep out the damn cold of bloody Winter. But the only room assured of a constant warm climate was the bedroom. Nothing more to be said.

In the kitchen. Daddy Bear had built shelves, but, on Mummy's Bear's insistence, he had made sure they were high enough so the greedy little fingers of Bartholomew couldn't get at them. Bartholomew's favourite honey was far up on the top shelf, a shelf packed with golden delicious eatables ready for the big thaw, rows of jam jars of all kinds: raspberry, strawberry, gooseberry, plums and pears, even figs and radishes, all just sitting there, waiting. But Bartholomew only had eyes for the honey pots. After all, he needed the vitamins, he reasoned, he was a growing Bear, they were not, you could tell that at a glance. Just a lovely sticky spoonful – he longed for it. The jars were transparent so Brian could see the yummy fruits floating inside. He longed to dip into them with both paws. And there at the end of the shelf sat his favourite - big pots of golden-bee honey, with the combs still inside, glutinous, shining, eternally tempting - all full, unopened, virgin honey! He wondered if he could he get his fingers under the lid, and into those super honey-pies? Surely he deserved it for sleeping so soundly for five months like a good 'baby Bear,' again distasteful words of the grown ups amounting to fibs! How he hated that expression 'baby' as if he was still in nappies and didn't know the difference between eating, stealing and defecating. Huh! He'd show them!

Perhaps… He stood just below the precious shelves and tried jumping up, but it was too far out of reach. His eyes lit on the sofa. He had an idea! He dragged it forward to just below the honey pots, then stood on the back and gave a huge leap forwards. His aim was to bounce high up off the springs in the bottom of the sofa, grab the biggest honey pot, then fall back, the succulent prey in his grasp. That was the plan. He leapt, managed to grab the biggest pot, but fell backwards, the huge pot was flung up in the air, the top burst off, and the whole receptacle came down with a thump over his head. The liberated honey ran down his face and neck and filled his eyes and ears and mouth. He could hardly see. By Appollo, he hoped his parents hadn't heard the crash. He groped for the front door. He had to remove the pot off his head, the honey off his body and the crime off his soul. Without panicking, he had the idea of rolling over and over in the leaves outside, to disperse the nectar. If this worked for combustible material, it was bound to work for simple honey. He had to hide the liberated honey-combs. If his Mum and Dad's eyes fell on them, there was little hope for him. He heaved the door open. It creaked a lot and he shot outside and hid among the hazel stands close by. Had his dreadful whippers-in heard him? He rolled about the leaves like a drunk grown up for a while. His little plan seemed to have succeeded, but every very inch of him was still covered with streams of luscious honey, which should have all been swallowed by now, but he still couldn't pull the spilling honey pot off his head. His feet, he had noticed, slowed down as he ran among the foliage, and finally came to a halt, as if they had a life of their own. He tried to move forward again. He couldn't, not an inch, his feet were heavy as lead, and his toes stuck together, as a single unit of foot. He was literally glued to the ground. Stuck as hell! Well , don't panic, he thought, after all, it is honey of the best quality, but how to get out of it, the pot still over his head, before the punitive primitives were roused from their selfish bliss, the swine, and move in for the kill, so to speak. Yes, he decided after a moment's thought, I know! I'll eat myself out of his one. He started on his fingers, licking between every one, but found the substance was so thick, he couldn't lick it all away. The taste nearly made him fall into a sucking frenzy. He positively gobbled himself up. Sublime! He had a go at his toes again and began sucking each in turn, but found he couldn't reach the little ones. When he stood up and tried to walk, the same thing, he found his feet were lighter but still sticking to the ground, so he had to shuffle forwards like a grizzly octogenarian. He tried to lick the honey off his eyes, so he could see what was happening but his eyes were half-glued shut anyway and his tongue, eager tho it was, was too short to reach them. His ears were clogged, his tongue couldn't reach them either. The honey just flowed on as thick as ever from the pot onto his head. He stood there like a slow drugged statue of a bear, without hope of budging an inch or two or seeing anything in the clear light of day. But, boy, was he ingesting! But before it got out of hand, he needed immediate assistance. He began shouting "Help, help!" but it came out as just a thick, flabby, flim-flam of belly grunts. Honey was clotting his gob and voice box, all the way down to his larynx. He shouted out to the badgers, "help!" he could smell them there. The badgers snuffled out of the undergrowth, but then just stopped and just sat and stared at Bartholomew in a mess. A touch of the old deserts for him?! The greedy snot-nosed little enemy was hoist with his own petard, drowning in honey of his own making. This was worth watching. The Foxes came out, too, sniffing for grub, but they too just sat and looked on, mere spectators at the great game of honeydew. Hadn't the thieving, bullying bears stolen the foxes' rightful meat and fine fare from under their very nostrils, every so often? No mercy now. The bunnies arrived and also sat in a row, and apart from licking their lips, stood shoulder to shoulder with the foxes and badgers. Things were getting dire. Again, Brian tried the licking game, but to no avail. At last he heard a scurrying sound. The foxes, bunnies and badgers were in a full circle of confabulation. Soon they all nodded in unison, which was rare. Bunny 1 came forward. Bartholomew tried to shoo him away but got stuck in the middle of a gesture, which means the end of gesticulation in these circumstances. Bunny began licking the honey off Bartholomew's toes, in between and in slow, light flicks; Bartholomew shivered all over, then laughed out of control; giggle, giggle - he was into a laugh a minute. Bunnies 1 and 2 concentrated on his nose; the foxes, his tummy, the badgers lapped their smooth tongues under his arm pits, up and down. Yes, the foxy plan was simple, not to eat Bartholomew Bear until he made his quietus with a bare bodkin, but to invite the ruffian on the stair to tickle him to death with an excess of mobile labia. Then sleepy Dormouse had been awakened by the cries of hysterical mirth, raging with hunger too, and joined in the lapping lickfeste. Soon all his forest enemies, and his Mum and Dad's too, were there - foxes, badgers, bunnies, hares, even weasels, all chuckling and chortling and licking like crazed banshees together, almost in chorus. Bartholomew felt tongues between his toes, hands, legs, arm pits and even on his own tongue in his own mouth, something very perverse about that, he thought dimly, wracked with fear of the fists of his far from effete Mummy and Daddy! Then a friendly swarm of older bees arrived. The Queen and Bartholomew shared one passion in life, - honey, dripping buckets of it, every day, all the time. Bartholomew shouted, "Help yourself, Queenie, take all you want, your family too. But release me! Let me go" After their communal honey grab and suck, Bartholomew hoped, he would be able to move his little fingers again, in acts of self-defence, if necessary. The whole army and navy of bees landed on Brian and gobbled up the yummy honey and in a few fabulous seconds, he could move his legs, and see again; he ran in circles, jumped up and down like a kangaroo, chased off those greedy bastards who had so treacherously pretended to come to his aid, the low forest menagerie of greedy buggers, he was back in the saddle! He ran his head into the oak tree, smashed the pot, and licked up the last remnants, going like hell, a victorious glutton if there ever was one, the swine of the greensward were not going to get what was rightfully his! But still all his antagonists still danced around him, licking him free of the last remains of the delicious stuff, and the bees did little buzzing songs of thanks for a terrific meal. But he could not shake them off. Bartholomew 's headlong smash at the trunk of the oak had woken up Mummy Bear and Daddy Bear. The door of the den was suddenly flung open. The ghastly parents stood there, looking puzzled at first, then furious. When they saw Bartholomew apparently being licked to death, they burst into rage, not at the cannibals but at the thief of the feast of their food, the brazen bloody Bartholomew baby! What did he think he was doing to their Winter sustenance, throwing it around as if was just ordinary conker jam? Never had they seen such unbalanced extravagance - giving succour to the enemy, laughter to the proles, and their stores to the voles and creatures of the dirty earth?!

Daddy Bear lurched forward and aimed a beefy cuff at Brian. It landed on his ear but there was plenty of honey left, and his hand stuck fast there, as it had with so many of the others at first. Daddy Bear tried to drag his hand off. Mum Bear joined in and together they gave a frantic tug, but the hand resolutely refused to come away. It stuck on the end of Bartholomew's nose. Mum had a go and her hand was instantly glued to Bartholomew's cheek. They all struggled to escape, and tumbled down in a sticky, barely glued-together heap. All the surrounding animals burst into loud guffaws - the slavering, gulping, hulking, idiotic bears had had their day. Their blooming reign was over. The nervous neighbours would never be blocked and bashed down again, the Bears' day of Greed had come and gone! All the assembled company paused to see what was going to happen next. Bartholomew stood ready to receive the coup de grace. With a huff and a puff and a final wallop at Bartholomew , Mummy and Daddy Bear held their heads high, under blushes of shame, it must be said, flounced off from their own once undisputed territory, their den, hands still stuck to their irredeemable offspring's bits of body, nose and ear, who saw the funny side of it, giving a wave and a grin of farewell to his finger-lickin' neighbours. The animals all jeered. Bartholomew knew that once inside, it might well be terminus time for him, however sweet it tasted. His long hibernation and short adventure might well turn into a permanent one! But deep down, he knew he'd just shown his Mater and Pater just what stuff he was made of! He'd survived and anyone who survived those two bastards deserved the Victoria Cross, with bar and extra honey! So there, bloody grown ups, especially the ones in your own house.

The Story of Cavendish and Clementina

Clementina settled down. She was lying sleepily among the tall swaying grasses, buttercups and the huge white daisies at the bottom of the field, next to the river. The first summer sun glinted on the gently lapping waters. No one could see her in her secret hiding place. She plucked a few daisies to make a daisy chain. The daisies were particularly big this year because of the rain. She suddenly heard a sigh and a rustling in front of her. Startled, but unafraid, she pushed aside the wild flowers and tufts of grass, and there, panting, sat a little being, he was quite tall for the tribe he came from, Clementina knew, and came up to her knees at least.

He jumped in alarm when he saw Clementina, "Ah!" he cried, "you gave me such a fright."

"What about me?" asked Clementina, "aren't I allowed to be surprised too."

"You're too big to be surprised by the little likes of me. You're three times my size."

"Who are you?"

"One of the Fair Folk of Iffland."

"You're a real pest. I haven't seen you before. What's your name?"

"Cavendish. What's yours?"

"Clementina."

"Why these silly questions on a glorious summer afternoon?"

"Why these dumps and frowns?" responded Clementina.

"It's you who've got those," said Cavendish testily.

"This is my den. This is where I'm supposed to escape to, not meet grumpy yob-goblins like yourself."

"That was a most insulting thing to say. I am no yob-goblin. What is your motivation for such nastiness? I know, you want to escape because you're going back to boarding school today and you're lashing out at everyone, especially people not your size. And your Mum's on the rampage, she's coming after you and she's got a rolling pin."

"That's for my Dad," said Clementina, "and he's gone into hiding as well. Anyway, none of your business, pest!"

"I'll have you know, I'm the Guardian of the Yellow Flags, the future Leader. The pestilence I leave to you. Hence my costume, you see, all shining like the sun, amber and bronze buckles, and buttercup-coloured tights. I love my little sunshine hat," Cavendish added, and waved it under Clementina's nose.

"Your buckles are tarnished, your amber decayed, your tights too tight, your sunshine too yellow."

"See those lovely tall iris-shaped yellow flowers growing like rushes in the water by the bank, see that hundred roomed palace beyond, that is my humble abode, my second home in the watershade, so what have you to say to me?"

"Must be noisy with all that gurgling water, and the colours are garish and disturbing," said Clementina asked, shuddering, "Who'd chose a bath house for a hidey hole?"

"Life is as damp as you make it," said Cavendish loftily, "there's always a welcome at the yellow flags for me and it's always dry as a bone. You simply don't know!"

"I know that yellow flags are wild Irises, so there."

"Cever, clever!" replied Cavendish sarcastically.

'Wait till my Mum gets a hold of you,' Clementina said to herself, "you boastful, jumped up, swollen-headed dwarf. Mum will take you down a peg or two, and your bleeding Irises as well!'

"Those grown ups of yours - ," Cavendish snapped, "your Mummy and her awful ilk! Why are they always so waiting to 'catch up on us and teach us a lesson' with a rolling pin, whatever those empty threats mean? What about them?'"

"I hate to agree with you," replied Clementina, "but reason is on your side this time."

"Why don't they drop their sense of hostility, throw away their rolling pins and leave us alone?"

"Life without Mum's rolling pins would be marvellous," conjectured Clementina. "Don't they know what we feel when we're waving goodbye at the train window? They'll never understand our tears, because they're tears of gladness. Hurray I say!"

Clementina and Cavendish exchanged a number of fives in total agreement. They were now in accord about something big, at least for an hour or two before the next outbreak of war, just like grown ups.

"But how can I help you, Cavendish?" asked Clementina, more out of curiosity than courtesy. Basically she was manoeuvring for the high moral ground.

"Daisies, Mayweed, Rosebay Willowherbs and Burdock, growing like crazy," replied Cavendish, "I can't find my way home through these thickets. They are so dense and tough."

"All due to the heavy rains," said Clementina.

"Oh, hark to the distinguished botanist!" said Cavendish, forgetting the temporary truce.

"You alright?" said Clementina irritably, "I'll take you home, just for the silence."

"I'm not supposed to tell anyone exactly where I live," warned Cavendish, "Grandma Yellow Flag warned me."

"Well, how can I take you home if I don't know where you live?"

"You're right, I suppose," said Cavendish, lapsing into neutral mode, 'I've got to trust someone, even if it's the grumpiest girl in the long grasses of the world. And you do not occupy the high moral ground, I do!' he thought.

"Piffle and ragwort!" exclaimed Clementina, knowing she was bigger and so would inevitably win. "Look at the size of my fists," she invited Cavendish, now backing off.

"If you were going to hurt me, you would have made a move by now," he said defensively. "War is the continuation of policy by other means."

"Clausewicz. Very crafty, you sneaky little copy cat," said Clementina , tight-lipped. "Don't mean a thing to me. Now where is this animal family-abode of yours so I can finally get you outta my hair?"

"Well," said Cavendish, co-operating under protest, "Lily Pond hard by Rushy Island. I can tell you that, but that's all."

"Don't worry," said Clementina, "I know exactly where that slimy slum is. Now shut up and jump on my back."

Clementina stepped out and walked with long strides over the giant daisies and wretched vetchlings, yes, they had kept Cavendish in his proper station alright. Wait till I'm on the high ground, Clementina thought, then I'll wheel out the heavy guns, and call up reinforcements. Mummy by name! Clementina came to a halt, peered through a curtain of Dog's Leg and Couch grasses, all tangled up with tough black Bryony. Before them now stretched Lily Pond with its Rushy Island bang in the middle.

"Hurray!" shouted Clementina, with fake excitement , "Home! -

the Slough of Despond dead ahead!"

"So, ta." Cavendish ignored the sarcasm. "I suppose I should give you give you some kind of reward." He tried to think of the most inconsequential gift he could give away from his box of toys and lead soldiers and could think of not one. But rubbishy old flutes – tons.

"Now close your eyes tight, and listen."

Cavendish took out a long, jet-black flute without stopping to think. He had planned to break it in half.

"Now, close your eyes!"

Clementina didn't want to do just that. She might well receive a boot up the butt or a blade in the ribs, you couldn't trust anyone these days. Cavendish raised the flute, and began playing. Clementina wished he hadn't. Cavendish played the kind of scales old tabby cats used in their caterwauling copulative choruses from wet rooftops, the sound traditionally strident enough to bend barbed-wire fences and strip leaves off trees. Cavendish wanted it to never stop. Clementina wanted it never to start. Cavendish could see, with immense satisfaction, how irritated he had made this semi-grown-up, bossy, pseudo harpy, immature Clementina. Cavendish wanted Clementina down and, if possible, out. Cavendish felt he was winning the inglorious battle. But he had got hoist with his own petard. He really could not stop the satanic screechings of the flute. The music transported him down, down into the lower depths of sentiment, among the strangled mocking birds, the dead doves and decaying upturned fish, of life, and farther and farther down still until he found himself gazing at the Portals of Hell itself, with a gang of dark Luciferic spirits on the other side, ready to persecute all comers at once upon arrival. There were no morals here, let alone high grounds of them. Had Cavendish been double-crossed by the spurious flute? Someone there definitely did not like him. They had switched him on and wouldn't switch him off. He struggled to stow away the flute, and finally surfaced out of the drowning, diabolic din, and saw emerge out of the treacherous, cacaphonic nightmare, a rotting ship the shape of a cowpat. It pushed off from the Island and sailed in their direction, but Cavendish now noticed, the boat was getting lower and lower in the water. 'What's this?' thought Cavendish, 'are they planning to drown me in the poisonous algae and block my true claim to be boss of the Fair Folk in the hard-won blood-bath battles of home? 'And what about this irrelevance by my side, this silly Clementina.' She would have to go. No doubt of it. He played it cooler than custard. 'Now big-butch,' thought Cavendish nastily, 'your reward," he said loudly, "just wish for something so hard and it will come true." Clementina shrugged, 'what an idiot,' she thought, 'dreams are for wood-peckers to come out the other side, not for human or sentient beings, who are forever on this side, in the dung and mud of huge perpetual death holes, the ignorant titch-bitch. But the titch-bitch decided to humour big-butch Clementina. "Wish like hell," he yelled. Wish again!" And he drew out his vorpal blade, and raised it over her head. Little did Clementina know that her suspicions had been absolutely justified. Death was imminent. She screwed her eyes tight and wished, and wished some more, and then some more. She was awakened by a distant vile screeching. 'What in the hell..?' she struggled out of sleep and saw the yells were coming from the direction of her house. She was fully awake now and still in her den by the river. "Clementina!" came the hideous cry, "Bloody Clementina! Time for the train ! Time to go! – thank god,' Mum added in undertones, "At once!" she waved the rolling pin just once at her sweet Clementina, and sweet Clementina know only too well her mother knew how to use it. The bullying, cutting voice echoed in her ears. She rubbed the sleep out of her eyes. No Cavendishes, no fair folk anywhere to be seen, no hells or damnations, no nightmares or floating cow-pats, far or near. Her wish had been for her Mum to come and rescue her hard, and she had got her Mum, hard. The 'music' had been so fiendish, Clementina knew her Mum was the only fury who could take on Cavendish and his devils, and liquefy them all with a single glance, melt them into incorporeal substances. She heard her Mum's final ululation. It rose above the sound of the Express train with 14 carriages as it rushed into the nearby station. "God, please," prayed Mum, "release me from the bondage of this recalcitrant tripe-hound, big-butch Clementina by name, Clementina the Detestable! My awful daughter!" She hollered sweetly again and flourished the battered pin with a crooked grin.

When Clementina got to school, the teachers soon discovered that their little monster had developed a deadly antipathy for all wind instruments, especially the flute. Clementina had immediately displayed her first bout of vile temper in the music room when she had been given the inoffensive little recorder to play. "Not on your Nelly!" she yelled, " Cavendish, out! Mummy, in!" and hurled Pan's pipe out of the window. On hearing of Clementina's dreadful, if enigmatic, invocation, all flutes and recorders were withdrawn from her reach and locked away. "Cavendish out, Mummy in!" remained her battle cry and hard wish to the end! And 'down with all yellow Flags' she would shout at every sun-set, like the Last Post! No one ever quite knew what she meant, but Mummy did, being the only one who had occupied the moral high-ground because she was the only one who possessed a rolling pin and knew how to use it. And you better believe it, buster! C'est la bloody vie!

Bernadette and the Sewing Box

One night Bernadette woke up feeling very thirsty. She did want a drink of water but she didn't want to be caught by her mother, who would invariably shout at her, "Pest! You've woken me up again. Back to bed and no water until morning." And stamp back to her bedroom.

So, Bernadette crept silently downstairs and went into the kitchen. She turned on the light, poured out a glass of water and gulped it down. When she was going back upstairs, she thought she heard a funny noise coming from the sitting room. She crouched down like a cat and peered round the side of the door. First, she saw her Mum's sewing box on the sofa, with the top off, as if someone had been using it. "Mum always closes it for safety and she goes mad about anyone who moves it,' she thought. "I'd better close it now." Her mother was like a monomaniacal warder over her sewing and knitting box. Woe betide any fool who might borrow a ball of wool or use a cotton reel without her permission. Mum was from Merthyr Tydfil, where the women are renowned for their foul tempers and possessiveness, not to say greed, like old grandma Bernadette, God rest her. Her Mum, too, was, to her advantage, built something like a square - squat, hard-edged, a lantern jaw and a wicked straight left. Bernadette glanced around nervously and pressed down the lid of the box but it wouldn't fit. She pushed with a will and suddenly the top slipped down hard, the box jumped up and reels of cotton, packets of needles and thimbles and showers of buttons, balls of knitting wool, scattered all over the carpet. "What have I done?" Bernadette whispered fearfully, "Mum's going to kill me with those fists of hers!" She tried to collect the needles off the floor and pricked herself. It hurt. She sucked her thumb, "how am I going to pick up all these things," she said, in despair, "oh, perhaps Mum is right, after all, I am hopeless, a hopeless pest!" Her Mum had boasted since her birth that poor Bernadette was the stupidest child she had ever seen, let alone, had. Bernadette rushed to the kitchen before any further catastrophe might happen and wrapped a wet cloth around her finger. Then she heard that funny noise again. She returned to the living room. A strange and wonderful sight met her eyes. A troupe of the famous mini-Fair Folk of Iffland tribe, not much bigger than her hand, were hard at work, playing games like mad. They had rigged up a trapeze with the needles and were swinging from side to side, shrieking with laughter. Others had built hurdles out of the reels and were having races. The knitting equipment had been re-constructed into a pole vault and the bravest folk ran at the looming bar and jumped, sometimes sailing over but often coming down with a thump! Others were even fighting duels with the needles as if they were rapiers and played game after game of tiddly winks with the smaller buttons. Others were hurling the bigger buttons like a discus. The heaviest Folk were having a tug of war. The teams often collapsed onto their knees, roaring with rage, but were cheered on to more savage tuggings after each defeat. Mum's thimbles were all lined up and a little folk person with a huge stone jar was pouring half-lemonade measures (I don't think!) into them. The Pixies stopped their partying from time to time to drink everything down, then dashed back to the games. The lazy ones had made sofas out of the pin cushions and were resting and snoozing. Bernadette looked at the mess. She knew who her Mum would blame. She, Bernadette would be hauled into the family court, her mother's, the first sentence - corporal punishment - Bernadette shuddered - then the second, the scaffold. Nothing could save her.

"Stop it at once," she cried to the messy beings creating even more chaos before her very eyes, but they took no notice and just kept on gambolling and may-dancing. She stopped the most active of the dancers, "who are you?" she demanded, "I haven't seen you before."

The Chief Folk person of Iffland, dressed all in red, and out of breath, said, "look, Baby, don't be such a drag. We're just being exuberant, it's our nature. And don't worry, Mum won't get your head, she's too precipitate, too predictable. We're careful as military commanders in the field. Every object is inventoried and its place noted in the grand scheme of things for re-placement if need be."

"Those are just vain, empty promises," said Bernadette , "no one can remember where all those things go. Only Mum can tell and for all that bedlam, she's going to have your guts for garters – she loves that phrase"

"Spoilsport. Cool it on the cat o' nine tails. We're having such a grand time, dish. And why are you wearing a bloody rag on your thumb? You don't need it."

He made a gnomic sign over the offending digit, reached forward and snatched the rag away. He was right. Her finger was whole, live again.

"Just like Lazarus on that single occasion," said the Chief, "no blood, man!"

"I can see right now that I will have to pay you much more respect in the future, which is OK with me, but my Mum will nevertheless haul me over the coals, and blame me for all her world turned upside down."

"No, she won't," said the Chief.

"Why not?" asked Bernadette.

"Because we are the Thimble Folk, too, the originals, warts and all, universally adored for our nimble fingers. You find us as you see us, dishevelled, sweaty, gasping, tumbling, bumping and clouting, but it's just being ourselves. After the dances and the games, we put everything back in its exact place, as I've just explained. When we've gone, it's as if we've never been."

"Bernadette, is that you?" came a loud, ominous voice from the top of the stairs.

"Goodness and gracious," gasped Pam, "my Mum. You'll never get everything tidy in time."

"O ye of little faith!," declared the Chief, "I know how to handle her beady eye and her deadly straight lefts, don't you worry. You go and make excuses to your Mum now, keep her out for a jot, just burble as you usually do, you'll see. Burble. Go on! " Bernadette reluctantly edged herself out into the hall. At the top of the stairs stood her Mum, left fist raised.

"What on earth are you doing down there, don't you realize what time it is? What do you think you're up to? Well, answer me. Come on, don't stand there like a fish out of a dish, stop gaping. Well? Have you nothing to say?"

"Just getting a glass of water, I think I'm doing that, round about midnight, not a fish, just a bewildered person, not standing, searching for the answers to life, and lots to blurb and blurb, cos' the red Chief told me I was good at that. I admit again and again too it was due to my desire for water, water everywhere, Mum."

"Red Chief!? Rubbish. Blurb? Right about that!? You, my

daughter have become a round-eyed nut-case round about midnight, I can see that at a glance! You're out of your tiny cranium, your cerebellum is melting like Spring snow, so go and gargle something, deep in your throat, then I'll hear what you have to say, and believe me the noose is tightening already, so give me clarity this time and I'll give you charity!"

"But I can't be executed without due process of law," cried Bernadette.

"In my house you can be executed without due process of anything!" Mum shouted, getting incensed about everything again. "So? Well? Come on? Why are you standing there like some hanged goose for? Silence at last. Is that what you're trying to say? No more honking! Are you trying to waste my time, part of my precious life, I could have been a Desdomonia, a Cleopatra - all on purpose, purposely to get at me. Is that you game?"

"I was just checking your sewing box."

"What?!" roared Mumsy, "you go in there in the darkness before dawn, and breathe all over my hollow precious thimbles. Prepare for the chastisement of the straight left!" – and she ran down the stairs, left arm already extended like a thunderbolt. Pam retreated rapidly to the living room and stood behind Mum's sewing box. To her utter astonishment the Chief had been right, everything was exactly back in its place, the sewing box even had its lid carefully closed. It really was as if no one had ever been there except, perhaps, bellicose Mummy.

"It's as if as if we'd never been here," said Bernadette daringly in, a red Chief voice.

But Mum was stone still, struck dumb, going through her

precious knitting equipment, checking every thread, speechless for one of the few moments in her life. She took a good hour to inspect all her sewing goodies, from needles to pins, occasionally looking with astonishment at her daughter.

"And I thought I'd left the top off! Well," she declared, facing her daughter, "the brain that organized this here has every particle of gray matter in its rightful place, every thimble in its corner, see, like little Jack Horner, almost surreal, every thread on its reel, every needle pointing towards true north; every ball of wool rolled towards the centre, I see it all now. The pull of the moon clouded your judgement at first, so you came down for a drink of water, but just in time, la lune pulled back to it to its rightful place and you with her, which is where I came in. Listen to me, funny tipped-over daughter, alles in ordnung!" She gave the Nazi salute. "Perhaps you're not such a hopeless pest after all!" - then as a good night gesture, Bernadette hoped, and one which shook Bernadette to the roots, she gave her daughter her a non-hostile close-up hug, even grimacing in the shape of a smile. And then terminated the interview with a masterly summing up, "all you were really doing at midnight just now, wasn't it, was just getting a glass of water because you were thirsty, am I right?!"

Demetrius the Dozy Dormouse

Demetrius the Dozy Dormouse lived with his sister, Cappadocia, and his Mum and Dad in a tiny round house at the bottom of a sheaf of wheat. There were lots of gaps in the walls and the wind whistled in whenever it felt like it, it seemed. This was another job Demetrius had failed to fulfil due to his chronic sleepiness. There were not enough feathers anywhere for comfort, the dry leaves had disintegrated and got in all their fur, the grass was now yellow and flattened, the fluff all straggly like lengths of old string.

The dormouse den was small and definitely uncosy, with only one little entrance you could hardly get in from outside, and it had kept them chilled through the entire Winter. Demetrius really was seriously sleepy. He had slept through all the thunders and lightnings of Winter, and now slept even when the fields shone with thirty degrees of sunshine in the summer. Today was a good one for being comatose. Demetrius's Dad and Mum had gone to market, after the crab-apples and crusts of bread which Demetrius had failed to pick up. Dad, the old autocrat, loved crusts and he always stole everybody's bag of goodies, and would eat them all up in the toilet. He only let Mum have the crumbs and apple peelings which she gobbled up before her son or daughter could get to them. Demetrius and Cappadocia were supposed to look after the happy home when the parents were out but this mainly consisted of little Cappadocia trying to keep her oafish brother awake with occasional kicks. The season was getting on and it would soon be time to harvest the wheat. Cappadocia and Demetrius were supposed to keep a sharp look out for Farmer George at all times, for he liked to get the corn in early. Demetrius felt nothing but indifference for his rickety home, in fact he loved anywhere he could sleep even for just forty winks, whereas his real 'home' was full of knit-pickers and rib-pokers. He was curled up in his downy corner, his tail wrapped around him for extra insulation. "There aren't enough places in the world for you to sleep in, are there?" said Cappadocia snappily, nearly tripping over her dozy brother and giving him a kick. But Demetrius just wrapped his tail tighter around himself and snored on, content with his lot. But prickly Cappadocia would not be put off by Demetrius's defensive measures. She gave him a running and jumping kick and yelled in his ear, "Mum and Dad told us to keep watch out for that bastard, Farmer George by name, the swine, he was up early this morning, tinkering with spanners, which is an execrable sign, Dad said so."

But Demetrius just snorted at her peculiar use of English and slept on.

Suddenly a huge rumble hit her ears and the filled the dishevelled den. She looked up in alarm. Was it thunder? A storm? A train passing by?" As it rumbled louder and louder, the ramshackle nest began to shake and quake as if it was going to fall to pieces Cappadocia could now hear the clanking of heavy machinery – yes! - the blasted combine harvester, right on their doorstep. Cappadocia scurried around, panicking. Where were Mum and Dad? In danger, no doubt. Had they got the food? Dad had probably eaten the lot. Mum probably nagging him to death even now. Was their straw shack going to fly up in the air due to the circular motions of the flayling machine? She kicked Demetrius for the tenth time. And he responded with his tenth snore. She dragged him out of his corner by his sleeping leg and dashed a glass of water into his face. That woke him! 'Clank, rumble and swish' she could hear as the terrible machine got closer. She would have to move, and quick, bugger her brother. She began tearing a hole in the back of the den.

"It's Farmer George, the swine, and his nasty harvester!"

Demetrius could move when his sleeping places were threatened, "he'll cut down on my rest periods and it will be death inside here," he yelled at Cappadocia.

"Move, Demetrius, you lazy sod," she shouted back, "Dad left you in charge! He always called you an 'otiose creep,' and he's right!"

'Clank, rumble, swish' went the harvester. Demetrius was at the door with a single leap. He peeped out and saw his chance. As the machine swivelled to turn, he dashed through the front door, with Cappadocia hanging on to his coat tails, "get off me!" he shouted, "you're dragging me back!" and gave her a few kicks to enforce his point. But Cappadocia was made of sterner stuff, and dug her fingers even tighter into her brother's coat. He dragged her along, shrieking in fear. Demetrius made for the bales of corn which were spewing out behind the harvester. They paused and looked back just in time to see the machine slicing through their little home and bundling it up in a hulking merciless bale "Oh," wept Cappadocia, "it was small but it was mine!" "Sentimental twaddle!" Davy snarled, just as his father so often shouted at him. Sue was immediately submissive and muttered, "wasn't taking to you, crappy dumkopf!"

"Follow me if you don't want to die," said Demetrius, "in here!" He wriggled his way into a loose bale of straw, waiting for the murderous George to finish off the field farther down so they could escape. But before they could say another word, they felt themselves being swung up into the air. "Oh, blast," swore Demetrius, "they're loading up the bales!" "Hell!" he turned on his sister, "your fault!" "Yours!" she spat back, "you were flat on your stupid back as usual!" He felt he could never comfort his sister again.

"I wonder if Mum and Dad got a boot up the arse as well," he said, "why just pick on the little ones, like us. Like me. I could stamp on that farmer George's face," he said, knowing it would have made little difference but he continued to work himself up into an ersatz fury , just like his useless Dad.

Again their little universe swung to and fro in the air, then it seemed to settle down and was still. The were parked somewhere. Demetrius wormed himself to the outside and popped his head out, followed by Cappadocia.

"Oh, shove your head out too, won't you," he said angrily.

"Be my guest" she responded quickly. At least that was one up to her.

They could hardly believe their eyes at what they saw. They were in a vast hall packed to the roof with bales, a wheat palace. And they were moving the bales out again onto huge lorries. Just as they looked, the next bale due for the lorry, stirred and out thrust Dad's head, followed by Mum's, both in frightful bad tempers at what was happening, and with each other. They promptly began exchanging insults, the usual sex war stuff, then started on the kids, "your faults, you hopeless offspring!" they chorused.

"No, yours, you hopeless mother, you infantile father!" riposted Cappadocia and Demetrius together.

" I'll have your all your guts for garters!" shrieked, Mum, 'you messy bits of old sperm! Don't you dare speak to your father like that!"

"Nothing to do with us," yelled the bro and sis again.

"All your fault, Mum," roared Dad, "I know where your dozy offspring gets his love of comas - from you!"

Cappadocia could not be constrained from sticking her oar in, "Your faults! Your faults!" - these words were exchanged a hundred times between the members of the dysfunctional dormouse family. The words dried up, at last, as they clambered down the stacks and scurried back to the ruin of their old homestead.

"That's it!" gasped Demetrius, falling inside through the wall.

"They'll never think we've doubled back," said Dad.

" Huh! - wise beyond your years, Pa!" riposted Demetrius sarcastically , "that withdrawal manoeuvre was my idea."

The cries of "my idea, not yours, my idea!" rose up again in a nasty, garbled almost human form.

Exhausted at last by their nocturnal exchanges, they settled down where they had been an hour earlier, in their shattered den, with its new fractures and fresh draughts, but this time Demetrius stood sentry voluntarily at the hole where the front door had been. He checked for any movement every five minutes. Animals he challenged first. Humans, he shot out of hand. From the turn of those ill-omened events, the hideous, destructive evil called the 'combined harvester', Demetrius never snoozed on the job again. Yes, he slept like a tree trunk, that was his nature, but never dozed, like zzz zzz zzzz, like a fool, an idler, a woozy sentry. Never! Demetrius the Dozy had become Demetrius the Watchful, for he alone now realised the real enemy was within. Yes, he decided, 'there's a curse on our family, we're all related.' It was the family which had to be watched!

"Halt! Who goes there!?" he shouted many times after midnight, even in his sleep, but only at members of his family! For the rest, it was silence.

Plumpton, Sebastian and Helburn the Horrid

Plumpton, the mongrel puppy, stood in the farmyard looking anxiously up at the sky. Black clouds were gathering. Was it going to rain again? He couldn't shelter in the barn because Helburn the Horrid, the demented farmer's wife, would sweep him out with the broom, or if she was in a particularly savage mood, with her hard knobbly old shillelagh. The Horrible One had a problem with time. She was old before it, she, who could have been mistress of all she surveyed, a star of stage and screen, a celeb, now going downhill fast due to her foul man's drinking, and this dead end of a farm. Whatever the regrets, Plumpton knew he was in trouble. He couldn't hide from the rain in the cowshed, too obvious. Helburn had it first on her list of last refuges. And what were the sows doing down there among the milch cows? Today, Plumpton thought, if the pigs were not at home, he'd try the sty, it stank to the lowest layer of slurry, but the host pigs didn't mind. Visitors often dropped in for tea and swill. In fact, the farm porkers welcomed newcomers, however grimy, anything to dissipate the shadow of the Horrid. Helburn wasn't socially enamoured of the piglet mansion, but it was something about the feeling of 'fraternity' there which messed her head. Yes, a soul as crazy at that!

The first leaden drops fell out of the slate-gray clouds and Plumpton squelched passed the short iron-gate into the pig-sty proper, small concrete cells, sloshy on all sides, but still cover from the storm. But once in, Plumpton was out! For Horrid Helburn was lying in wait. She had already chased out the superfluous porcine householders. They had scampered, in terror to the cow-field and hid themselves among the bull rushes. Helburn now rose up out of the pig slop, a towering muddy spectre, a prodding stick in one hand, an electric cattle-goad in the other; by her side, a bucket of watery slops for the porkers, on the other, a full pail of what appeared to be wild hazel nuts. Horrid Helburn was a natural punishment of nature with eyes like a hawk. She spotted Plumpton in a second "Don't you dare hang about here, you dirty mongrel," she yelled, "this place is too good for the scabby likes of you. Out! Out! Out!" She shrieked her usual curses, "you scabrous immigrant dogs, all over the shop! Pomeranians , Irish Mick Setters, Scotch Jock Terriers, Taff bloody corgies, a real plague there, they can't understand English, bloody Hun Alsatians, hairy Afghans, you are all just international syph scavengers, wogs incarnate, nauseous four-legged contagions, you are mothers and fathers of rabies-babies by the score! And those Tory hounds, too, upper class vermin, baying through here, I'll shoot the lot and throw in the fox too, for free, next time! What about the old English Sheep-Dog Trials, noble animals, highest of the Anglian breed, never mind the royal corgies, can't understand them, I just said! And now," she frothed on, "you multi-deformed mutts of casual birth, you inglorious bastards born of drabs in ditches, the undeserved punishment for our pains, out, out, out!" She went for Plumpton with the electric goad, of which he was terrified, but he managed to slip out of the iron gates before Helburn could slam them shut.

"You're not even fit for the most neglected sewers of Mogadishy, Africa, you degenerate, skewbald orphan!" she yelled, throwing fistfuls of pig waste after him. She hated mongrels beyond all reason – probably because she was a bit of a bastard herself. But she could never be quite sure. Hence the tempestuous outrages. And Plumpton made it worse by always being equally bad-natured, however frightened, and sometimes even exchanged blasphemy for blasphemy. His pretence of geniality was so complete that other animals sometimes avoided him. He quickly ran though his expertises - dishonesty, openness; slyness, charm; sulleness, cheerfulness - stupid contradictions which he knew irritated Helburn no end - how she loathed paradox.

Plumpton dashed through the rain to the old oak tree in the middle of the yard and crouched down for shelter. Was Sebastian the Squirrel at home? A fine little fellow but an acquaintance rather than a friend. Would he take mercy on him? Streams of water began running down Plumpton's neck and he shivered. In a few moments the water would find its own level and there would be no shelter here. He knocked, not once, not twice, not three times, but more and still more, at the concealed entrance behind the bark. Only Plumpton the Mongrel could be so persistently intrusive, Sebastian guessed. Plumpton now heard quiet foot-falls. Sebastian's secret little door slid open.

"Hell," he said, "you still out here, you should be drowned by now. "

"Help," yelped Plumpton, grovelling convincingly.

"No," said Sebastian , "I don't want you in here wetting my lovely carpets and stealing my Winter food. Don't come on in at all."

"What do you mean, 'stealing your food.' I've never done that, tho I admit I've tried often enough."

"Thief!" retorted Sebastian, "I am never going to usher you into my little den and let you dry yourself off with a towel."

"Come on," said Patch persuasively, "I mean, your food...?"

"...yesterday I'd collected my Winter hazel nuts and left them in the roots outside and when I came back, they'd gone. Who would do a thing like that?"

"I am no vegetarian, Sebastian, I will eat anything on order, from chestnuts to custard pies, OK, but the blame for that heinous theft cannot be laid at my door, because I have no door."

"But with your sense of smell you can sniff out a hundred odours close at hand, right?"

"...hang on, I've got it!" Plumpton broke in abruptly, holding up a paw, "I know who stole your precious nuts."

"Who?" demanded Sebastian, "tell me now or you're out."

"I'm not even in yet. Let me in first to enjoy my creature comforts away from this black-browed storm and then..."

Sebastian cautiously let him in.

"Now! Out with it. Who stole my hazel nuts, my life-giving kernels?"

"It was horrid Helburn,. I just saw her out there, holding two buckets, one full of swill, the other full nuts, for the pigs!""

"Never!" shouted Sebastian.

"I saw it with my own eyes. It was horrible," said Plumpton, stoking up the ire.

"Hazel nuts are far too good for pigs," yelled Sebastian.

"She's just doing it for spite."

"I'll starve this Winter," said Sebastian, suddenly blanching, "if I'm not careful."

"And I'll drop dead of malnutrition," said Plumpton.

"We've got to do something. We're dry in here alright, but that's no good if you're still hungry. Think!"

"I need sustenance," said Plumpton, "to think."

Sebastian reluctantly brought him an old ham-bone left-over in a corner. After a bit of much needed nibble, Patch slapped his paw on the table, "She's always after me, right? I mean chases me like hounding me, she thinks, but in which situation, it is *I* who am actually leading *her* a merry dance.

"Well," enthused Sebastian, "let's do it that way then, with a purpose, a praiseworthy motivation more than justified in the circumstances!"

"I'll expose myself, dash across the yard, then pretend I'm lost and I've got nowhere to go and dart off away from the nasty sty, leading her off the beaten track, yes, ... then you can..."

"...nip into the pig-sty with my bag..."

"....and steal the rest of the nuts back before they're all gone!"

"You're not so insufferably wrong after all," Sebastian muttered, but sotto voce - not to give Sebastian any hope for shelter in the future. But they shook paws on the deal. Sebastian grabbed his bag, and let out Plumpton into the pouring rain. Plumpton at once set to howling and whimpering and running in circles in the middle of the yard, chasing his own tail as if his last days had come. Sebastian hopped out over to the roots and scuttled off to the sty and hid by the little gate until he knew the ogress was not at home. The reaction to Plumpton's antics was not long in coming. Horrid Helburn leapt out of the sty. She had been hiding in ambush all along, waiting for the counter-attack. But Plumpton's antics provoked a blind wrath. She dropped her pail of reeking stuff and intact nuts, and waving her shelaleagh, sloshed through the mud after the crazy pup. But Plumpton was brisker than the heavyweight harridan, and literally began running circles around her. The circles got narrower and narrower, until Horrid Helburn had been lured far away from the heroic mongrel's next pail of food. At that moment, Sebastian nipped out from his hiding place, grabbed the discarded rations, and dashed back to the safety of the roots of his castle, entered and slammed the secret door. Outside, Plumpton now changed direction, as planned, and rushed back in a straight line to the bulging roots where succour lay. Sebastian was waiting. As soon as Plumpton had darted inside, they barred the door. They listened, grinning fiendishly at the locked portals. Harriet had missed Sebastian's courageous sortee, and was now searching the sty again, completely off the scent. They could hear her intolerable hollering, "Come on out, you dirty unforgivable mongrel, I'll report you to immigration! You don't stand a chance, you're so ugly!" They heard her voice getting closer and she began hammering on the tree trunk with her goad and staff of office, shrieking curses not only at Plumpton but at the world as well, about not being a ballerina, but all to no avail. Her footsteps faded for a while, then a renewed explosion of temper , much louder than before even though it was more distant, for Horrid Helburn had discovered that her nutty feast had disappeared. She re-doubled her hammering on the locked tree trunk in the rain, "My hazel-nut sweeties," she shrieked, "who's got them? If it's you Plumpton, you are a dead dog! If it's you, Sebastian, say your prayers now! You're sick with disease, both of you, and the proper authorities will hear of this. The Hygiene Department will give you hell, like me, you two despicable down-and-out felons, robbing an old lady of her all. But I promise you, I'm not called Horrid Helburn for nothing!"

Hrrid Helburn's imprecations were greeted only by the sound of flowing water and the muted grunts of happy mastication. Search as she could, she could not find a single nut anywhere, nor one secret doorway, nor one culprit either! Inside the den, the two bastards, all discord spent, differences made up, for once, shook hands and came out chewing, the full sack of nuts lay between, with all Winter to enjoy them.

Meanwhile, on the outside, the terrible storm continued, with horrid Helburn right in the middle, ululating in defeat to the end!

Tarkington and Titheredge
and the Circus Hamper

Tarkington and Titheredge were talking about the circus they'd visited the day before. They were standing outside Titheredge's family semi on the outskirts of town. They had just finished their daily, ghastly mind-blowingly pointless academic chores at the local Comprehensive Futility. Titheredge was proud of his parents' achievement in possessing such a mansion, three up, two down, while Tarkington curled his lips in contempt, "think it gives you class, do you? Never. My Dad's a foreman."

"A foreman who gets drunk every night habitually."

"That is a damn lie. Put up your dukes if you don't deny it, mate!" Tarkington bristled.

"Don't be truculent, mate. Let's stick to the point."

"I wasn't being truculent. My Dad's as good as yours any day. He's always telling me watch out for your uppity class manner, that's 'not worth the snot up a beastie's nostrils,' that's what he said and by god, he meant it!"

But Titheredge knew he had won the exchange as soon as Tarkington had raised his fists and began quoting from crappy American films. Tarkington's Dad was well known as the local, lower class drunk. He had been appointed foreman for sucking up to the union conveners and to the bosses too. He was a natural two-faced working class hypocrite. "Every community has one," Titheredge's

Dad had said, "so you can place the blame fairly on his shoulders. But keep quiet about it. Be sly. Everybody knows anyway."

Thus, thought Titheredge, had his father exhibited his superiority in every way, especially in terms of class. Titheredge's Dad was upper lower class, Tarkington's was lower working class. 'Be sly,' he thought, Dad was right yet again. Everyone knew. So he, the Prince in Waiting, was next in line. Bugger Tarkington, he was down and out already. Titheredge smirked, his was the higher calling every day!

"It was a bloody good circus in spite of the Animal Protection Warriors, is what I meant," said Tarkington.

"I agree. Dead right. Green shits do not a barrier make!"

"Not so loud," said Tarkington. Look."

Titheredge was pointing at the two Green warriors they had seen interrupting the circus the day before – very distinctive, Titheredge thought, with their pencil moustaches and Crocodile Dundee hats. The friends hurried on.

"But I gotta admit, that tiger had the longest teeth I've ever seen," said Tarkington, "and the longest snarl this side of hell, man."

"The elephant was the biggest bone-crusher this side of Brooklyn Zoo, Tarkington, and had the longest nose I've ever sniffed, man," said Titheredge, mollifying his best mate with agreement.

"Let's go down again to Brick Meadows, bound to be some stuff left behind," said Tarkington.

"And the bits and pieces will have been snapped up by the Brook Street boys."

"But it will be fun to remember all those horses in their snaffles and the girl acrobats in their blue tights," said Tarkington.

"OK, Tarkington! Gimme five, man." He got five. 'Duped gain, the pea-brain,' thought Titheredge immediately. Tarkington squared his shoulders, he was leader of this little gang, head of the receipt of fives in the community, and his Dad was the main man on the block, no doubt of it.

They walked down to the big Brick Meadows, so called because the bog estate which had been there had collapsed due to bad building practices, like undredged sand in the mortar. The walls had begun cracking and tumbling down on their own volition. The brazen squalor had finally been razed on the spot, and the broken masonry left to rot and grow Fireweed and Loosestrife, so the site was useless for anything except visiting itinerant crappy circuses, the odd staggering Emperor butterfly and was already a heavenly dumping ground for worn out sofas and fractured fridges.

Tarkington and Titheredge surveyed the whole sorry wasteland of ruin and sterility with eyes emptied of any expression, except possibly those in the look of vultures picking over burst black sacks in search of discarded peelings, half-chewed grizzle, fatty rind of pork chops, myriads of little garbage heaps in themselves, all of which meant nothing to the two T's. After all, the stuff was there every day, a well known local landmark, like the town hall. The clean, bare patches were where the tents and cages had been, the marks still quite visible, tracks where the huge ten-wheeled lorries had driven on and off, leaving the soggy ground churned up with brickbat tracks and dangerous ridges and potholes.

"That's the way they went," said Tarkington pointing at the tracks to the main gate of the field.

Yes, thought Titheredge, 'it is lovely to remember the fun moments of the past' – I don't think!' But he let the thought pass. He didn't want to make his mate any more inferior than he already was. And there'd be far better opportunities to humiliate him than this.

"Look," said Tarkington pointing as they approached the overgrown ditch outside the gate, "what's that?"

They walked up to the object, half hidden in the long, dank grasses and weeds.

"It's a ...hamper!" cried Titheredge.

Untold treasures after all! The Brook Street Boys had not pillaged properly. The two anti eco-guardians pulled the hamper out of the ditch.

"It must have fallen off the back of a lorry," said Tarkington. Titheredge looked at Tarkington and Tarkington looked at Titheredge. Mates were they!? Huh! Titheredge motioned to Tarkington and Tarkington lifted the lid slowly, once again confirming his leadership of the threadbare tribe, as it did Titheredge's Dad, the hegemony of the area. They stepped back, but no need to worry, for inside quietly lay the Tiger Tamer's braided uniform, all red and gold, with its row of medals, and silver buttons all down the front, a holster at the belt. The Tiger Tamer's long leather whip was curled up by it. Underneath they found the long scarlet gown and billowing nylon pantaloons of the Elephant Rider, his turban, a peacock's feather and a bright paste jewel in the centre. And at the bottom, mountains of blue girl tights, still very sexy. Tarkington shoved Titheredge aside, grabbed the Tiger Trainer's costume and put it on at once, as if in the vanguard of the circus procession. The costume was far too big and he had to hold up the trousers with one hand, but he felt strongly that he was alongside his Dad, a true boss of bosses, the formidable son of the Boss Tiger Tamer of all time.

He had forgotten poor old Titheredge, who looked on with considerable envy. But Tarkinton suddenly grinned a real mate's grin. 'Be sly?' Jesus, he did declare, hadn't his Dad once argued that his boy he was for the Diplomatic Service as well as being a leader of the Boy Scout Movement! Tarkington imitated the action of the Tiger Tamer, clawing the air, biting the wind, growling like a hungry croc, inciting attack! He cracked the whip, 'crack, crack!' it went and Tarkington could almost see the Tiger launching itself fruitlessly against the whip- lashes of himself, a Master of his Craft. It was even more fun doing it, than remembering it, he thought. Poor cowed Titheredge was still at his side, still pretending to grin. What a nerd!

Titheredge, not to be outdone, put on the Elephant Tamer's costume; the pantaloons came up to his shoulders, and the turban down over his eyes, but the purple cloak flowed majestically behind him. He recalled the braying, snorting, subservient trumpeting of the elephant to its Master, the Great Titheredge! He cupped his hands and made the harsh, irresistible calls of a wild bull Elephant in musht.

Tarkington, at once not to be undone, cracked his Tiger's whip. 'Crack, crack!' and the noise merged with the braying, half human, elephant calls. Suddenly they both stood transfixed, staring at the shape which was emerging from behind the thick hedge. First, two sharp, furry, ears perked up, followed by a moist snout sniffing for food, two blazing yellow eyes in a huge head afterwards, then the brilliant striped back of the big tiger, top of the pride. It paused and gazed at the shivering pair. "It's the whip," said Titheredge, "you'll have to crack the whip." "No, I won't," said Titheredge, white but determined as any a minor idiot, "don't tell me what to do!"

"He's staring at the whip. Crack it!" Tarkington stuck to his convictions, give him that, the berk. Titheredge seized the whip, jerked it back, then hurled it forwards into a huge double "crack, crack!' And the Tiger took a long leap through the air, as if through an invisible hoop. Tarkington cracked again and again the tiger jumped.

"It thinks you're the Tamer," said Tarkington, "he's so wrong." He snatched the whip back. "I gave him the first crack of the whip, so the fame of taming the tiger in the wild belongs to me!"

To reveal the extent of his derision, Titheredge gave a series of roaring, blasting elephant calls. "Hah!" he shouted at Tarkington, "the authentic calls of the Jungle Book! Call me Mowgli!"

He wished at once he hadn't quite put it that way, for a mini-mountain seemed to be being born upwards in the bushes and the King of the Jungle, Big Jumbo Juventus, the Elephant Leader, strode forward to where the terrified Titheredge stood. With one sweep of its mighty trunk, Jumbo swept up Titheredge and placed him carefully right on top of his huge, bony, bulging forehead. Then – Jumbo paused. And so did the top Tiger, both behemoths, in their own way, waiting for the next order. All four stared at each other. But Titheredge knew they couldn't stay like that all day, in frozen postures of near shitting themselves. Tarkington wished they had never even seen the blasted hamper. It was Titheredge's fault, he was convinced. His Dad would settle his hash. He had never opened the hamper. It was Titheredge again. Then, in the distance came the scream of police and ambulance sirens. God, thought Tarkington, 'we'll end up in the cells now.' 'Be sly! Nothing to it, Dad!' thought Titheredge. Two police cars screeched to a halt. Out got four hefty cops, and after them, Titheredge's Dad and Tarkington's Dad, already gesticulating wildly at each other. Ignoring the tiger and elephant, they promptly turned on the most terrified of all the animals, their dumbstruck, trembling sons. Meanwhile the clumping heavies were spreading out, keeping law and order.

Titheredge pointed in alarm. Up on the hill a platoon of Animal Protection Warriors stood, with mixed expressions - satisfaction at the discredited humans, and approbation of the nobility of all animals. Not a drop of chagrin anywhere, the self-satisfied prats.

"Bastards!" growled Titheredge

"Coppers' narks!" responded Tarkington.

"That silly swab of a son of yours!" Titheredge's Dad roared, "he led my boy astray!"

"Never!" shouted Tarkington's Dad, "your milksop of a son couldn't follow a baby baboon. Hey, whey-face!" he called out to Titheredge. Titheredge's Dad bridled terrifically.

"Your class is lower than that of a Traffic Warden's! A dustman is king to you!"

"You piss-artist of the ages! Stuff your stupid semi and three-piece suite, this is all your fault."

"Yes, your fault!" cried the boys, following their fathers like lemmings, all pointing accusingly at each other. "He opened the hamper!"

"No, he did, your fault!'

"No, he did!"came the cry again and again. It echoed over the de-forested hills and bare mountains. The Animal Eco-warriors turned their backs, victorious Zulus to a man, raised their arms in farwell, mooned just once, and faded into the heat-haze of an African afternoon.

The circus workers who had arrived in their ten-ton lorries, alone did their job as laid out in the works' schedule, with deft movements and quiet resignation. Ignoring the family rows, and in the face of considerable constabulary imbecility, they recovered their four-footed charges and vivid costumes. They at once split the pad, quit the joint, man, in silent disapproval. The Peelers were still trying to keep the lower-in-the-scale sons and fathers in some kind of generational and social order. When the class-war was about to come to blows, the bluebottles, models of impatience at such importunate times, arrested all four of ' the noisy bastards' for affray, causing a public nuisance, cruelty to animals and for being irretrievably lower class. At the station, the bloody recriminations and choruses of "your fault!" continued well into the night, typical of all those who do not regularly bless their Squire and his relations. Meanwhile, the circus, with its devoted prolaterian workers, its top, bottom bosses, its lone tamers, retired in good order, a model of non-confusion, men who knew how to keep their proper stations. The entire cadre bid adieu to the field of battle and retired fulfilled to a man, man, plus a happy ending for animals like Tiger and Juventus, everywhere.

Hecktide the Great Dane

Hecktide the great Dane lived on the Royston-Smythe Estate, north of Hampstead, but still near the centre, and Primrose Hill, with all its celebs. Hecktide belonged to a good, old fashioned county-gentry family. There was plenty of room, acres in fact, for Hecktide was huge. His head was as big as a horse's; his teeth were as long a tiger's; and when he yawned, his mouth grew big as a cave. When aroused, his voice was like a thunderstorm directly overhead. Everyone was afraid of him. He looked so fierce and his bite seemed more atrocious than his bark. But unbeknownst to the general run of the posh neighbours and their innumerable 'honourables,' poor Hecktide was an emotional cripple. If anyone or anything lived to define the word pusillanimous, it was the gigantic Dane. It was well known among the animals on the Estate that Hecktide had been worried almost to death by a dormouse, who, while terrified of the slavering canine head in front of him, held his ground, but Hecktide had taken off, howling, tail between his legs and took weeks to get over the fearsome encounter. Added to this chronic tendency to timorousness, was a hopeless sense of direction. He would sometimes walk in circles trying to discover where his body began, and always ended up facing the wrong way.

Hecktide's closest friend was Ingrid, the Master's gorgeous Swedish au pair. She had understood the moment Hecktide backed off the meaty ham bone she had offered him on their first introduction. Any Great Dane who backs off in fear of a lithesome giver, when offered a juicy hambone, she knew, must possess a primordial squeamishness, a vestigial funk, or, more kindly, somebody who was no stranger to rapid strategic withdrawals, who waked backwards into fights - in short, a shitty , secretive, cupboard coward who had never come out. But being full of the Swedish milk of human kindness, Ingrid never mentioned this to anyone and so Hecktide and Ingrid became best buddies. If a stranger gave them even a passing glance, Hecktide would dash and hide his head in Ingrid's skirts, "What a brave doggie,' people would say, "one look at her and off he rushes to protect her vital parts. No one is going to get past those tweeds, however voluminous."

Once, as Ingrid was setting off for a quick tryst after school, some of the randier boys began shouting filthy accusations at her, making motions of removing panties, and advanced their crotches at her. When Hecktide appeared, the rocks began flying, and Betsy shouted to him "Run, Hecktide, run!" and Hecktide, already half way to a straight-jacket, out of fear, promptly bolted, with his eyes tight shut, his jaws wide open, gulping down the air like an athlete afraid of coming in second, as he fled. But he had got the whole situation back to front and was galloping in the wrong direction, N. N. East, and not N.N. West. Instead of running away from the beastly little boys with dirty imaginations, he ran directly towards them, his neck reaching out, after his prey, surely, his jaws agape, dripping with saliva. When the ghastly little yobs saw him, they came to a full stop, scared as shit, man, and looked for a way out. It a second they had turned and ran full speed ahead of the rushing Dane. Both parties were now going in the same direction, fear making them all very fleet of foot. The scabby urchins, scared out of their paltry wits, yelled, "A beasty, a mad beasty! Help!" and they ran back to almost to the school, the universally detested Comprehensive intellectual slop bucket of all ages, such was their yellow streak. Ingrid yelled to the Hecktide, "Come back, you idiot, I am where you always want to be, behind my skirts. Here, boy, here!"

The   people   who   had   witnessed   Hecktide's   inordinately courageous action in chasing off the offensive louts, all broke into cheers. Thus was added yet another legend to Hecktide's life. "But," Hecktide sobbed as Ingrid stroked him later, "Ingrid," he all but whispered, " What am I going to do? I can't even run away properly. Will I ever be able to do something brave in the right direction, all by myself?" "You will, Hecktide, you will," Ingrid promised with a slobbery kiss.

Ingrid on the way home was very careful to lead Hecktide through the field which contained the Estate's prize bull. It was now or never, she had decided, Hecktide, her best pal, simply had got to shed this lamentable cowardice stuff, and get a sense of direction in his life for once, kill or cure, and that was why Hecktide was now plunged right in the caca. As they came round the corner of the great central oak tree, the next thing Hecktide knew, he was confronted by a raging, bull, pawing the ground, tossing its horns, ready to charge through any oak tree or Hawthorn hedge in its path, to do the last dirty on the most timidest unGreat Dane of them all.

"Run, Hecktide, run!" cried Ingrid.

Hecktide shot off like a bullet on legs and ran - straight into the hedge - and began thrashing out, trying to release himself, and his fear, from the sharp thorns. The bull saw the commotion but not the cause of it, so burst through to the path in a confused and nervous condition, afraid of the unknown threat in the hedge. He looked around for his unseen adversary. Nothing. He bellowed to the skies. Nothing again. He edged his way back through the hedge, showing the white's of his eyes, he could also be as timorous as a dormouse, when he wanted, especially since he believed in ghosts, and those shivering motions in the bushes were surely caused by sullen spectral bodies, preparing to drag him by the ankles to some unspeakable death. Hell, he whirled around, the invisible furies were after him. Hecktide looked on from the far side of the hedge, joy spreading over his face, for he had done it, he had run deliberately, albeit accidentally, at the immense beastie, in the correct direction for once. The only stroke of fate had been the hedge encounter, which he could not quite fathom, but it had done him an unexpected favour. All this action, for his pneumatic Swedish Ingrid. He yelped with joy as he saw the tossing bull, ears flattened, tail covering his arse, galloping and taking shelter among his silly heifers under the oak tree.

Hecktide lolloped over to his proud mistress. She had surveyed the whole scene like Boadicea of the Iceni tribe at the sack of Colchester, yelling her approval and shaking her abundant blond locks to and fro. Her grand design had worked, Hecktide was really now the local hero, Great Dane Hecktide indeed!!

"You are the greatest, bravest Dane of them all!" she said, kissing him wetly. "You see, Hecktide, you did do something brave, and you did it in the right direction, all for someone else, that someone else called 'me', for all to see! That is courtesy far above and beyond the call of duty, far above King Arthur and his Lancelot, for your very own Stockholm Ingrid, for love, of me!"

And, thus, Hecktide and Ingrid remained approximately together on the posh Royston-Smythe Estates near Hampstead-on-the-hill, for many a day - indeed, for long after all the primrose ways had been plucked. There is a plaque even now on the hill of Hampstead which commemorates the victory of the Great Dane, Hecktide by name, over himself and his overseas love, Ingrid.

The Amazing Gig of Batty, the Scatty Cat

Batty the Scatty Cat was settled in to his place in the hedge at the bottom of the garden. On the far side was the cow pasture but the cows were sheltering under the single oak, for protection against the blazing sun. Sherhezade, their leader, though, looked calm and cool. The geese and ducks around the pond floated in the shadows. The two ponies, Hippolyte and Martingale stood up to their hocks in the water, the only way to keep cool in the heat wave. Batty lay with his two best friends, Tug and Mitford, sleek, healthy pussies, in the flattened brown grass, yawning and purring. What a stunning, mind-burning sunny summer's day! Batty suddenly stood up, cupped his hands around his mouth and let go a series of high yodelling notes, like a Swiss shepherd to his charges in the mountain meadows of the Canton de Vaud. Tug and Mitford started in surprise. Batty had given no warning. They were not amused. Not a day for noise, they thought, except perhaps for the sound of snoring.

"Hey," said Mitford, the Siamese with a monocle, "Will you kindly desist, Batty," he said looking down his nose.

"This is not the kind of day for screeching," said Tug. He was called 'Tug' because both his ears had been torn off in a fight one night. But Batty yodelled on.

"'Please desist,' said Mitford again.

"What's 'desist'?" asked Tug.

"To stop, to cease, to dry up!" he said loudly to Batty.

"I could drink up a whole pail of milk," said Tug, holding up the empty bucket.

On the word 'milk', Batty changed his tune. He belted out an aria from a famous opera, as if he was the prima donna. He swept up and down the hedge as if in search of an invisible well-oiled middle class audience. His friends looked on in alarm.

"A touch of the sun," observed Tug.

"Go comatose!" Mitford declared to Scatty, polishing his single glass, "you'll crack my monocle."

"Batty," said Tug, "you mad catty Batty, I have no ears for your song. In fact I have no ears at all." He roared with laughter as if he had said the funniest thing in the world. But Batty wouldn't stop. He carolled onwards like a loon.

"OK, then," begged Tug, "Then give us some honest rock and roll for a change, not that Covent Garden caterwauling stuff!" and covered what was left of his ears with his hands. How he hated opera, all those fat people with bad breath, false notes and full wallets… "

"…or at least a towering excerpt from Bob Dylan," put in Mitford.

Batty calmed down at once, for Bob Dylan was the god of the melodic scale, like Pythagoras, not to say of poetry as well, to would-be songster pussies everywhere. But this tight-lipped silence of Batty was rare. Then they saw which direction Batty was staring and they knew the reason for it. Batty was gazing longingly at the empty milk bucket. They exchanged glances in a trice, licking their lips. It was not difficult to see what they were thinking.

The sudden beat of rock and roll shook them out of their reverie. It came from the top room of the farmhouse. Taliesin, the farmer's son's favourite number, was playing "Roll over Beethoven," which he and his top cats adored. 'Davy,' as he was formerly known, had changed his name after seeing the Welsh eisteddfod on TV just once. He was now signing himself 'Taliesin of the Shining Brow', a famous bardic name of the Demetian tribe. Taliesin was their number one 'people' friend in the farming community. Batty grabbed his air guitar, frantically swivelled his hips, and ran through some of the most famous riffs in the globe, Hendrix foremost among them. He then belted out *Rock around the Clock* like the hedge was host to a top rock n' roll super star, with enough room for all his myriad fans. Then Batty switched into his cowgirl adoration attention mode.

"That mad catty Batty thinks he's a lonesome bluegrass cowboy," said Tug.

"Completely insane!" said Mitford.

"What's 'insane'?" asked Tug.

"Round the twist, up the wall, bonkers…"

"…I get your drift," said Tug, "I'm not as denuded as you think! You're bonkers!" he yelled at Batty.

"I've been like that since birth," admitted Batty, "and my parents loved me for it. But," he added, pointing at the bucket, "the words on the tip of my tongue are - 'a raging thirst for the white stuff!'" The friends fell silent. The single question in their minds was, "How to fill an empty bucket full of the milk of human kindness?"

"Leave it to me," said Batty. He stood on the highest point of the hedge, directed his guitar towards the top room of the farm-house, the source of all its Beethoven, and prepared himself for song.

"One thing about that mad Catty," Hippolyte remarked to Martingale, looking at him on his high hedge," he really does try…"

"…and he never wants to ride us, like to the Hunt and dressage and all that prancing stuff."

"I hate all those bridles and snaffles," said Hippolyte, "Batty knows just what we feel. He's like that. He loves rocking to ponies."

The geese cackled their agreement, "and he doesn't try to eat you for Xmas out of bed and board, like the rest of the humans, the sows and boars."

In unison, the ducks expressed their approval. "Exactly right!" and added for the benefit of slow learners, "and he can be really funny…" "…and truly musical," interjected Mallard , the leader of the quack pack. The cows strolled around the water's edge greedily supping up the water, regardless. "One thing about Batty, he never tries to take too much of our milk with that greedy old milking machine," said Scherezade, the top yielder of the tribe, "and he never sneaks up on us like a typical feline," chirped in Gramatica the Blackbird on a bough above, "and he can carry a tune, no doubt about that!"

"He can be a scream sometimes too," said Martingale to everyone. All the animals and birds of the air now stood around the pond, enjoying the cool, still waters, and the elevated chat in a rare exhibition of true fellowship.

"Watch him go, man!" suddenly yelled Hippolyte, pointing at Batty who was going into his final rendition of the greatest music of a lifetime. He rock 'n rolled, man, like Elvis at Vegas; jived like a master jiver, jitterbugged like a jitterbug gladiator; did three Michael Jackson moon-walk routines to a 'T' and finally collapsed, breathless, his tongue hanging out. His friends looked on with respect at this enormous expenditure of energy, admiring Batty's near perfect Detroit sense of rhythm. This was a cat, a batty catty, mad perhaps, but a true cat nevertheless underneath it all, especially gifted in the higher regions of musical point and counter point. Unanimously, Tug and Mortimer decided to come to the aid of their breathless, hip-swivelled, supernova star. After the briefest of consultations, they decided to put their plan 'B' into immediate effect. They grabbed the bucket, formed the cows into a circle, and gave the original version of 'Roll Over,' not so badly either. The cows mooed and swung their udders in time – music can produce prodigious amounts of milk – if properly applied, it's well known, and this occasion was no exception. A huge bucketful was soon taken most willingly from the swingingest dairy herd in the land, especially from Sheherazade, the biggest producer and fanatical lover of Ludwig van. "Practice makes perfect milk," she swayed in response to their compliments.

They all now approached Batty who was just recovering. His eyes grew wider when he saw the slopping, sloshing bucket. This time Tug and Mitford didn't try to blare out the chorus of any song, everyone would have covered their ears anyway, so they merely bowed to Batty and offered him the entire bucket, wholesale, "To Batty, and the whole Batty, and nothing but the Batty," said Mitford loftily, making the sign of the twelve-stringed guitar over him. But Batty impulsively embraced his dearest friends, they had done him proud again, and at once beckoned to them to share in the white frothy ambrosia before them.

"Ever generous," murmured Scherezade, "he deserves every drop he can get, any time, on my slate."

The three friends dipped their tongues into the bucket, then began lapping furiously, all meaowing, contentment herself. Batty whispered to his friends with a satisfied smile, "Who says Catty is batty now?"

"No one ever said such a thing," declared Mitford, inspecting the milk through his monocle, "the only thing I've ever heard about Batty is that he is pure genius."

"What's 'genius?'" asked Tug.

"Genius," said Batty purringly, "is a cat with his head deep in a full bucket of milk!"

And as if in recognition of this famous summertime gig came more of the wondrous *Rock Around the Clock* from Taliesin in the farmhouse. He had watched the whole of Batty's amazing gig from the window, and now punched the air and waved triumphantly to him. The animals cheered and returned all salutations. Yes, if, but for a moment, perfect harmony had existed between man and beast, all thanks to a mad Cat known as Batty (and his rock 'm roll guitar) but, as I see it, 'Batty' was anything but that! For once, the milk of human kindness had spilled over.

Plummer the Polite Pigeon

Plummer the Polite Pigeon had come up to London from his green bower deep in the Sussex countryside, and found himself a visitor to the world famous Trafalgar Square, opposite the National Art Gallery. He toured the monument, noted all the fighting going on in the pediment of the immense pillar and statue. For a moment he felt a stranger in a strange land. Nothing like this ever went on in his part of England's green and pleasant meadows, save the proles, on, say, a Saturday night - so far from this shrine to Britain's martial glory, hardly believable. People never even grimly accosted each other in his manorial village, let alone blew off each others' heads.

Plummer stood on the rim of one of the fountains. He felt he needed the touch of clean water, for it seemed to him, the paving stones of the area were a mere flattened muck heap, spread with antediluvian grime, bits of eternal sticky plastic wrappers, with huge blobs of blackened chewing gum underfoot, crammed with bugs, bacteria and loathsome infections. But he noted there were hundreds of people feeding the myriad pigeons in all directions. These birds were quite forward in their demands for a bite of something and when frustrated, fought like the silly sailors on the plinth - as it were, over something which could never come back

Plummer felt faint after his long flight but when he tried to peck at a bit of popcorn, he was invariably ousted by one of the big city pigeons, fat and foul and aggressive. He noted that next to himself, the man with the kindly face was feeding his flock out of a bag filled with very large crumbs indeed. Plummer also saw that the man offered sustenance only to pigeons who had exceptionally good manners. The behaviour of some of the pigeons was sometimes quite reprehensible. Plummer watched as a troupe of pigeons descended on the man. First, they pushed each other out of the way, then pecked at the crumbs, both in the man's hands and in the bag, and followed this up with a quick gobble, then a scramble, only to come in again like stuka dive bombers onto Soviet airfields at the beginning of the '39 war. "Shove, snatch, bomb and gobble!" is it?" said the man as he whooshed off a dozen ill favoured pigeons at his feet. "Not a morsel for you greedy, pushy, misbegotten, destructive little mittel-european, immigrant sods!"

"Excuse me… " said Plummer.

The man immediately responded in a very courteous way, "Did I hear 'excuse me' before my very ears? Aha, a pigeon of immaculately good manners, I trow. What is your name?"

"They call me Plummer at home, sir."

"Sir?' Did you say 'sir'? How wonderful, how nostalgic, just like little Lord Fontleroy! Bless all Victorian little boys, 'angels of the hearth,' they called them. I bet they call you Plummer the Polite Pigeon at home, or a phrase something like that. Good to make your acquaintance." He shook Plummer's hand warmly, but not familiarly. "Do you often come up to town?'

"Only in exceptional circumstances, sir," replied Plummer "without undue emphasis on the 'sir,' "which I try to avoid."

"Of course! Me too," asseverated the kindly OAP, "and I can tell from your accent that you went to a very good school, a public school if I'm not mistaken. Ah, the old courtesies, Edwardian to a 'T' after the 'Victorian 'E'. 'Please' and 'thank you' at the drop of a hat! 'Sir' every day over devilled kidneys at breakfast - yes, 'sir', an excellent thing in pigeons. But social conditions have gone from worse to much, much worser. Over there on the corner was the great upper class clothes emporium called 'Moss Brothers,' 'Moss Bros' for short. It made uniforms for all the officers of all the imperial persuasions of the West, which were many in those dear far off days. Then the materialistic axe fell, bloody war – what a spoil sport, just a stupid global binge really, money no object! and what is that magical Moss Bros now? A Tesco's, a lousy branch shopping joint! A sandwich bar now stands where Major Generals decided the fate of nations, on their own initiative. Moss Bros was also the hub, club, nub and centre of the best families of pigeons within the very covers of Burke's Peerage, their whole manner, as well as manners, a perennial delight to behold. Now where are they, these remnants of a once well-mannered age? Look around you, see our noble refugees, our impoverished feathered friends, our displaced honourable pigeons, our bewildered but elegant upper class of migratory birds, such as yourself, trying to find a place in the sun and a finger bowl at the banquet before they die. All replaced as you can see in front of my toes down there," he kicked and whooshed off more of the glutinous infamous immigrant-petitioners, "By God and Victoria!" he cried out, "by all the louts and loutesses, the yobs and yobesses of the present pleb epoch, begone, I say, begone!"

He turned again to Plummer, gesturing to the unruly feathered mob before him, "They may be plump, they may have money sewn into their wings, they may have half-Essex estuary accents - wotcha! where every man is, 'mate', mate, but you can always tell - manners maketh pigeons. 'U' and 'non U" still obtains in the Home Counties, I tell you. So Polite Plummer, finish off these crumbs you never even begged for. Super to see the old politenesses hold sway even for a second, especially in the glory that was Trafalgar. You will find me here every morning, serving crumbs to friends. And Plummer, I am inviting you to have breakfast with me every day, until your business, whatever its tenor, is successfully terminated. Good manners are not only a virtue, their reward is always crumbs, crumbs, crumbs all the way." As Plummer finished off the crumbs with great satisfaction, he knew now too that in the grim and stained plinths of the current age, there were still a gentleman or two left, here and there, just, in the green and pleasant land of Rule Brittania!

Caractacus the Duck and Piscator the Pike

Caractacus the Duck was not an old duck but neither was he exactly a duckling. His feathers weren't quite grown out but no one could mistake him for a youngster. His father was Monsignor Drake the Elder, the local bigot, but genial with it. The Monsignor was proud of his son but was overly strict with him. He was always telling Caractacus that he was on the point of adulthood and that it was time to take his new responsibilities seriously – like talking in gruff tones, glancing at panty lines, etc, etc. Dad always urged his son, "to grasp the bullet, my son, bite the nettle," but he said this every morning after a breakfast of health-giving cereals, when Caractacus could give no feed-back. Very unfair timing, he thought. Caractacus often got fed up with talk of 'testicular transition' whatever that meant, and his Dad's instructions, although he loved his Dad, especially when he was absent. He couldn't help wondering whether his Dad had forgotten that he too had gone through this abysmal 'change' and had suffered similarly, presumably, in spite of his high hierarchical rank . Had the memory of those ghastly night-time emissions eluded him in old age. He had heard otherwise. He felt he knew just as much as his senior citizens about growing up, and he wasn't even gray. 'Just give me a chance,' he thought, 'I'll win my spurs, you'll see, I'll cast the perfect bait!' He was thinking of his Dad, his holy position in the firmament, and all his perpetual pontificating, when he, Caracatcus, was down at the river that May morning. It was a slow river with lots of swirling, deep places under the banks; clusters of bull-rushes, flowering pond weeds and even some golden globe flowers were scattered about the edges.

Caractacus liked exploring this region. He called it his Safari

Adventure Marsh , and he ventured farther and farther into the reeds every time he went. It was such a lovely spot to play in, flat, private and gurgling, with few, if any, of the ghastly fellow humans, he was supposed to put up with every Sunday at confession. Caractacus couldn't imagine any dangers lurking around the flowing bends. On this super blossoming day in May, he waddled farther out into the stream than he had ever waddled before, quite gaily and without any feeling of responsibility at all. Surely his father was exaggerating about that. He parted some shining pond-weed and peered ahead. His foot touched something, making a gentle clanking sound. He looked down and there stood his father's rod and reel, and a big oil-drum of bait, huge fat worms wriggling there, awaiting their fate on the end of a hook. They did look so very inviting, for Caractacus loved a meal of those elongated, creeping delicacies too, particularly the ones in the river bank just here. He sat down, dipped his bill into the writhing mass, and gulped and chewed and swallowed until the lot had gone. He didn't worry. He knew there were plenty more ready for the plucking. He found the big tin drum was now empty, and for a bit of fun, he hopped into it, and sat like the captain of all he could survey, comfortably. The mill race farther down was quiet today, enough water under the bridge, no sweat. He settled down for a snooze. Why not? after the heavy snack, he deserved to doze off. Suddenly he felt as if he was spinning around. He rubbed his eyes, and sure enough, the tin was nudging into the main stream, swirling round and round in the current. Caractacus stood up abruptly when he felt his bottom getting wet. He looked down and saw that the tin under his feet had worn thin and water was seeping in through the pitted, rusting metal. Caractacus wasn't worried. He was a fine swimmer and could paddle to shore in minutes. No problem! He was about to launch himself overboard when a long dark shadow passed under the sinking 'boat.' The water stirred and for a moment he got a glimpse of a horrendous gaping snout with its rows of sharp teeth glistening above the surface. He couldn't venture into the water with that beast lurking around! The homicidal fish was famous the length of the river and was called 'Piscator the Pike,' voracious eater of tiddlers, frogs, and even stray duck chicks, a varied menu and it conveyed just the right tenor of Piscator's bloody existence - he lived to eat, and ate to live. A monster of indifference to the sufferings of smaller animals and bird life everywhere, his voracious appetite was never satisfied, morning, noon and dinner time. Caractacus felt a definite thrill of fear, it was getting to be dinner-time for the deadly Piscator, and fast. Then Caractacus realised he should have hearkened to his holy old Dad and his sacerdotal wisdom, and not ventured so far from their home in the tall mace reeds and duck rushes. He should not have forsaken his responsibilities although apparently it was all tied up with silken thighs and ejaculate material in sleep. Had his Dad really forgotten about all that? Had he spent all his feelings on God? What about his children, forgive them for they still know not what they do - the body is the bloody mystery of the holy Ghost, all right!

Just then, something nudged the drum and it floated a little farther away into the current. Caractacus saw a snapped-off tree-trunk floating past. It was trying to push him towards the bank. He stood and cheered, the Green Man, the guardian spirit of the woods, had come to his aid. He was safe now. But no sooner had he thought that thought, the optimistic fool, trying to accept the responsibilities of what he had done, the bobbing branch swept into the 'boat' and sent it spinning into the centre of the stream again - which stream was now gathering speed, faster and faster. Caractacus could hear the roar of falling waters as they approached the old mill race. Caractacus was now confronted with a triple deadly threat, the waterfall, the shadowing pike and the broken branch - all seemed to be conspiring to bring him to a sticky end and the termination of his responsibilities, still only faintly apprehended. He prayed to all the gods of nature in the Garden of Eden above, and to Ystragal below, to come to his help. He was too young to die, too responsible now! Suddenly from the weeping willow on the near bank, came a frantic quacking and a rush of wings, and Caractacus saw his agitated, worried father-figure swooping above him. Monsignor Drake was a pretty big duck, of unusual size and strength, with a voice to fit, an impressive sight at any gathering. With a mad flapping just as the boat was about to plunge to its doom over the waterfall and its foolish occupant devoured by the merciless predator, Pa Piscator the Pike, Monsignor Drake, caught the edge of the sinking container in his bill, and flapping his wings like mad, created a following draft, and finally succeeded in tugging the boat to the far shore. "Jump out!" he shouted, "you cheeky sod, kiss God's earth, and face up to your new duties and responsibilities!" Caractacus hopped out sharpish. He noticed that there was just one inch of leeway left, and that the vessel was fast disappearing into the frothing, murky waters, followed by the dangerous branch, still poking at its doomed prey. The hideous, ravenous Piscator the Pike had darted away up-stream, looking, no doubt, for further 'thoughtless irresponsible little victims like you,' as his father so aptly put it. But Caractarus was being driven half mad by the repetition of the word 'respon....' and spat onto the bank to show his sense of boredom and rebellion.

"See," said his father emphasizing his point with thunderous quackings, "Pike the Piscator is off now looking for further fodder - which means thoughtless little semi-mature ducks like you! Listen my son, I call you 'son' in spite of all the virtues of the sacred crosier, I am human after all, you are on the point of grown-upness and you nearly messed it up. But God be blessed, you have not been chewed up in your extremities!" he looked around. " And my bait. Where's my curling juicy morsels gone? I bet in your tum-tum. You hog, you greedy, harmful hog! Am I right?"

"Yes, Pa,' Caractacus caved in one hundred per cent, he was up a gum tree! "I did wrong, all of it, I didn't take my dawning responsibilities seriously enough, I'll face up to any bullet from now on, I will bite on any projectile, roll in nettles naked, say confession about night sweats every day, overcome any impulse to go on safari! I swear I have learned my lesson. I really have, I mean, the snapping teeth below me, the branch poking me in the ribs, the mill race ready to swallow me up, you bet, Monsignor Dad, I will always in future bend a ear to your guff, your spiritual advice, your Apostolic bent, I promise. And to make a start, and to demonstrate my sincerity, I will replenish your bait right now." And he began digging into the soil on the bank with a will, pulling out delicious, rotund specimens, and placing them in a pile at his pleased, and parental Confessor's feet. Caractacus was putting on a most convincing show.

"From now on, Pa, I will always consult you before any venture into the undergrowth of life."

Mr Drake nodded, and made the sign of the cross over the worms, content. He saw his son didn't really mean it this time again, but the hypocrisy had been well nigh perfect, and had stood steadfastly by him, a much needed help in time of trouble.

What a holy reconciliation was there! - father and son brought together by near calamity, cemented again by holy Mother Church's blessing, all in the common family quest for tasty wrigglies and widespread virtue – and God's Vicar on earth reinforced in his power! - a pretty picture on the muddy banks of life when all is said and done! Vive la famille!

The Victory of Tadema the Tortoise

Tadema the Tortoise was sunning himself on the outcrop of rocks just down from his home in the garden. He had taken two weeks to get to this spot, but it was worth it. The grassy, stony mound was a favourite with his friends too, but they could catch the fast train, on foot! Swinehead the Snail was Tadema's best friend. They could see right through each other, and didn't mind what they saw – a rare example of blind person-to-person 'I-don't give-a- damn,' which was OK. Tadema looked at his fellow creatures down in the next field - badgers, foxes, rabbits, so many quadrupeds, that sort of ilk. He watched them at their strenuous exercises preparing for the Daddy Long Legs Black Rock Sprint, and was always amazed at the unending sense of competition they exhibited, "all that wasted energy," he said to Swinehead," so unnecessary! All you do when you've won is go back the way you've just come and do it all over again, and get angrier and angrier, whether you win or lose, until people get so envious, someone is killed. Why not just join us and bask in the slower facts of life, throw the hurly burly out of the window and look on the world as we serene tortoises do, like me, and snails too, why not?" Tadema wasn't being superior. When he stood still, he could do so for months and months and never feel tired. He and Swinehead Snail were really the happiest creatures on the mound. Swinehead whispered something to Tadema who seemed immediately astonished, as at a very wise saying. Swinehead pointed at the feverish competitors below and whispered, "Why travel miles to talk to strangers at great expense when you can stay at home for nothing and talk to your best friend – yourself?" Tadema nodded. Not quite germane, but getting there.

The final weekly races were about to take place. The badgers, foxes, weasels, rabbits, hares, had gathered in so-called friendship and harmony for a bit of fun, but they had a low opinion of Tadema's speed, and Swinehead's lethargic gait, and were just waiting to say 'no' for their entry to the races. Each competitor had every intention of expressing their disapproval of the anti-social exhibitions of Tadema and his foot-dragging mucker, the stationary Swinehead. Chillingham and Thornton, the twin puppies who peed all over the track, regardless, were already in shorts and running boots, now approached Tadema.

"Tadema," said Chillingham, "come on, join in. Jump over the sticks, run in circles, sprint among the buttercups, this is the Daddy Long Legs Black Rock Sprint. Join in and run like mad, like the rest of us."

"I mean you live here," said Thornton, trying lying sweet reason, "you're entitled to."

"The world would turn upside down if people didn't exercise their rights," said Chillingham forcefully.

But Tadema shook his head and Swinehead nearly dozed off.

"Doesn't anything get you going?" asked Chillingham.

"Lettuce," said Tadema quietly.

"You're an old slowcoach," said Thornton, "why you're even afraid of taking on Swinehead the Snail right here by your very side."

"Don't you talk about my oldest friend like that," said Tadema. But Thornton had found a tender spot.

"Cowardy custard," he and Chillingham chorused.

"Say no more, "replied, Tadema without a single rising inflection, "you're on."

"You really will enter the race?" asked Chillingham.

"The famous downhill sprint," said Tadema with conviction, "the All Animal Annual Spectacular? From the top rock? Yes! Swinehead the Snail here will be my manager, coach, masseur, medical adviser and psychiatric Aide, OK"

"OK!" said the astonished twins and relayed the news to the waiting participators and spectators, who gave shouts of muted approval and murmurs of scepticism. At last, the top decent meadow folk had succeeded in persuading the nonconformists, the non-conventionals, the slowest elements of society to do their social duty and join in with the Dionysian revels of the majority and rush around a bit.

Tadema and Swinehead exchanged faint smiles. They knew what to do by just looking at each other, it was said.

The race started up at the top of the mound. All the athletes had gathered there in a line, with Tadema in the middle with Swinehead at his side. Maxentius, the badger raised the starting pistol. Swinehead at once went into top gear, no messing around, high gear from the off. Swinehead at once rolled his partner onto his side so the rim of his shell rested on the ground. Tadema in fact became a tight little ring of tortoise flesh, bone and carapace. He stood there on his side, held up by Swinehead, a hardened hoop of wrinkled manhood ready for the fray. Everyone laughed at first for they thought Samuel was resting his friend up just for a quick doze but had fallen asleep on the job. How wrong can athletes get, even top hop-skip-and jump champions, who knew their shallots!? At the very second the gun went off, Swinehead gave his friend one almighty shove. Tadema immediately started rolling down hill like an unprecedented avalanche, speeding ahead, bumping and jumping and rolling and never losing his balance, gaining speed every second, before the others could get their breath. Tadema at last bounded over the finishing line, a triumphant human wheel, ahead of the whole square field. The population of the meadows cheered in surprise and delight - trust them, the hypocrites - the two 'anti-socials' had joined the merry gang and had taught them a lesson to boot, namely, 'let sleeping snails (and tortoises) lie!'

Both Swinehead and Tadema, though they might have had the slowest legs in the community, had the fastest brains. No one ventured to invite them to participate in the overblown rigours of silly Olympian exertions again. They knew that Tadema and Swinehead were the unchallenged champions of the Daddy Long Legs Black Rock Sprint, the annual Animal Spectacular, for a very long time.

Bibiena Bunny and the Great Escape

Bibiena Bunny was playing on the deserted railway line. His mother had warned him not to, but Bibiena questioned her every order now. Why should he not? He hadn't been born yesterday. He came from a line of exceptionally gifted bunnies. His grandfather had been the leader of the pack and had fathered a huge tribe of bright tufted critters. One had been personal locksmith to the Queen Mother, another an inventor of universal keys to very tricky, rich furniture. Both bunny pre-eminents had performed feats of nonconformity, and were permitted to live in the grace and favour burrows by the railway. With this distinguished history behind them, how could his Mum always cry wolf, thought Bibiena. He would show her! What was Mum thinking of? What were her last nagging words? "Don't lose the magic bronze key. Put it on a string around your neck." Bibiena hesitated, "Just do it!" she ordered. Bibiena slammed the door when he left. Didn't he always wear that splendid key around his neck? Didn't he adore it? Wasn't he proud of it in company? To defy her, although she could not be seen for miles, he climbed onto the bridge rail and walked across it. He paused as he heard 11.15 goods train coming. "Lovely things," he cried out. How he loved trains, big ones, small ones, fast ones, slow ones, funicular ones, Orient Expresses ones, but this one he fell in love with at first sight. Why? Because it was red, red all the way, from top to toe, every hub of every nub was painted in scarlet and vermilion. He craned his neck down to get a better view. His first real rouge-atre train, tender and locomotive with blood-coloured goods wagons, open to the skies, with trunks and suitcases strapped onto the vivid, blushing roofs. It was precisely at this

105

moment that Bibiena took his eye off the whizzing, tawny miracle below him, cheered - then slipped off the rail, and fell like a clod of clay, down directly into one of the open wagons. In a second he became entangled in the tarpaulin covers and ropes and struggled to find a way out. He could feel the train accelerating, clankety clank, clankety clank, faster and faster. It hooted as it dashed down the hill, farther and farther away from home, and yes, his Mum too. She didn't seem so bossy now! As he tried to clear the canvas cover off his face, he felt a hand gripping his ankle, then it pulled like mad. Bibiena at last could see again. He was under the tarp and sitting outside a cage. In that cage was a monkey and that monkey's hand had reached through the bars and had pulled him to freedom.

"A million thanks," he said. "Hang on, you're a monkey."

"Yes, and proud of it too," came the reply.

"No doubt," replied Bibiena going out of his way to be polite, for hadn't his Mum always said "be not forgetful to entertain strangers for thereby some have entertained angels unawares?" His Mum seemed more and more right - clankety-clank, clankety-clank - but was this an angel? No, it was a monkey, a very friendly one, that was a given, which would have to do for the nonce.

"My name is Mirador," said Mirador, "and I perform tricks wearing a silly gold braid uniform and tight black silk trousers - which I hate."

"I'll hate along with you," said Bibiena, "because I hate what I'm doing now, riding on a train into the unknown although I adore trains."

"Destinations aren't always unknown, " Mirador opined, "we're all going to Frankfurt-am-Main, to the new cage and cell centre for performing beasties, like me."

"Shameful," said Bibiena.

"Ask all the animals here, there's one in each wagon, an elephant, hippo, alligator, boa-constrictor, stick creatures, all the usual suspects, and yes, even a cage of bunnies, but they are for supper, and they will all agree with you – shameful!"

"Maybe" said Bibiena, "but those fellow bunnies are not for supper - if I have anything to do with it!"

"What's your name?" asked Mirador.

"Bibiena."

"'Bibiena' is funny for a bunny."

"Not if it's the brightest Bunny in the family."

"Prove it."

"I am only lost but you have been captured. I am outside but you are inside. I live in a bank, you exist in a cage."

"I know all that," said Mirador testily, "but what can we do about it?"

"Isn't it obvious! I have to help you to escape – 'why?' you might ask? Well, because I have a plan all ready, already, and it must not go to waste."

"What about yourself, your life situation, your fate thereof?" asked Mirador.

"I want to go home, because that's where I want to be free. Nothing to do with my Mum or the family, just me!"

What's the plan?"

"Wait for the next steep grade or stop for diesel. Then I will then uncouple the couplings."

"But we're all locked in."

"Believe in angels," said Bibiena taking the key off the string around his neck. "This is a universal family key á la Bibiena, like Faubergé," he explained, " brilliantly conceived by engineers of the miniscule in my family, not only does it unlock your common or garden padlocks, it opens the very doors of paradise if you so desire and are courteous enough not to despair. A doubting Thomas do not be!"

"Goodness, this uni-coloured, most uncommon train is slowing down already."

"I told you I had a plan. My dear Mirador, I will release you first. Now follow me." The incredible bronze key had soon done its job. They were now both well outside the cage. The train shuddered to a halt. "Uncouple along with me!" ordered Bibiena. And they did. In a trice, all ten wagons had become loose cannons. The animal populace scattered along the lines looking for their braveheart leaders. Bibiena with Mirador had performed a world -changing beasty feat. Yes, a mere section of the caged folk of the universe had been freed in a second and for all the good it did do, it had also hit the world headlines. What followed was a holocaust – of cages! Cages everywhere were never the same again, exposed as they were for what they really were, a real let down! They were devoured in fiery furnaces often, fed by the former cheering inmates.

Bibiena now yelled, "Geronimo!" and gestured ahead. His happy followers headed for the nearby wood, the supper bunnies bouncing up and down cheering their new Chief. How they welcomed an angel unawares! "No more bunnies for tea, no more bunnies for tea!" they chanted merrily. Lead by Mirador, while Bibiena headed for home, knowing his Mum would be pleased with the way in which he had honoured the family name, so she wouldn't nag him ever again - the escapees penetrated deep into the darkling wood. Well concealed in the wild Guelder rose bushes, they decided on the next phase of their master's plan - with Mirador at their head they would march on the Town Hall or Rathaus of Frankfurt-am- Main. And they did. But did they win the huge engagement that followed? Take the crimson train to Frankfurt-am-Main immediately and find out for yourselves. After all, you are as free from cages as they, or me, aren't you?!

Marsden Moretaine and the Feat of the Red Wellington Boots

Marsden Mortaine had a diabolical squint. He saw things in twos and sometimes even in multiples of three's. He wore pebble-lense glasses with heavy frames, but this was to cover up the affliction rather than alleviate it. As for his age, he had just achieved double figures and was jubilant. But he continued to stumble, totter, topple, tumble, blunder, slip, perform frightening glissades all the same. He watched his feet as if they were about to run off all by themselves. But the compensation for this loss of focal vision was remarkable. After much practice after school, his sensory detection of close and distant objects was phenomenal as radar. However he still remained blind to the quality of the object and the danger it might pose.

At last, the final test came. On the Sports Day at the end of the summer term, he found himself standing at the start line of the last round of the famous National Junior Schools Obstacle Race. His school mates to the right of him and to the left, offered no favours, and were poised ready to do their utmost, if not during the day, then certainly during a Night-of-the-Long-Knives, later. If Marsden Moretaine's vision was as perfect as Galileo's, what difference did that make to his well being? Look at what they did to poor Galileo ?

Marsden Moretaine's genial old Sports Teacher, known as 'Onwards!' from the off, stood beside him, arm outstretched, "ready, steady, Go!" his starter's pistol barked its command. Off went Moretaine like a gazelle - and after five paces of galloping out of control, fell flat on his face. 'Onwards' helped him up. 'Such a debacle for young Moretaine again,' he thought, but said, "Well done, Moretaine! You had such a go! Now, onwards!" Moretaine could have hugged him. The kind words cancelled out months of humiliation. Moretaine crouched down again, staring somewhere in front of himself, ready for action, at any angle.

"Onwards!" shouted 'Onwards', and once again Marsden shot off, but tripped over bunches of knot grass after only a few steps, and fell, losing his spectacles in the tall ragwort.

"There were at least a dozen molehills in front of me," he complained later to 'Onwards', finally locating his glasses.

"And tomorrow, young Moretaine?" queried 'Onwards.' "Neverthless," said Moretaine with gutsy verve, "I shall be here at three for your race, come heather or high water! No question of it!" But I'm sure I looked really silly in the short grass," ventured Moretaine, peering though the pebble lenses.

"Everybody looks really silly in the short grass," responded 'Onwards', "especially from a prone position. Give it your all and miracles can happen. Look at me. Look at my situation in life, look at my physique, my rounded shoulders, my narrow chest, my rickety ankle bones, but, at the same time, note my nonchalance in the face of adversity. You could get to be as successful as me! Got it!"

Moretaine loved his old teacher, he was at least fifty, had bow legs, a spindly body and was chronically short of breath due to chain smoking. His fingers were yellow from nicotine, but still no one found this unique person off putting. 'Onwards' would enter the class room, blow his nose into his handkerchief and inspect the contents with minute care. When satisfied about something in the snot-rag unknown to the class, he would nod and replace the soiled linen in his top pocket. He would then mesmerize the class on whatever topic he happened to hit upon. He wore a faded hacking jacket from the Charity Shop; a tie which was stained with a dozen egg yolks, marmalade bits stuck to his old pullover, and coffee stains on his shirt. Pyjama bottoms peeped out from the legs of his trousers. This was because he often slept in the staff room overnight and couldn't be bothered to change. His face was covered with shaving cuts and his beard grew straggly and yellowish. Yet Moretaine and everyone else in the school knew that this man was a winner, the most popular teacher, with the best results every year. He was the man everyone knew would occupy the last space for a plague in the school hall. Even outside school, people raised their hats to him. Although he looked like a tramp, thought Moretaine, 'Onwards' really is a great man. What matters a fiendish squint in life, he thought, or multiple points of view every day? "They are as nothing!" he said out loud 'to 'Onwards's' disadvantages, I will follow that man until I reach the winning podium like him and raise my fist in defiance of the world of disabilities!" Yes, 'Onwards' was the man to imitate. He was the total exemplar, a tiger of the old school!

After the debacle was over, Moretaine, for a change of scene, went to the magician's booth of the visiting fair in the Town Park. He loved the Magician's tricks, especially when the he walked through the wall, or promenaded up the sides of his caravan - another perceptive freak who saw a future for Moretaine and was not put off by his multiple, simultaneous points of view.

As Moretaine was arriving at the Magicians', he came upon two men at the rear window of the caravan, trying to prise open the lock. Moretaine at once rushed inside, warned the magician and rang for the police on his mobile, (a gift on arriving at double figures of age.) After the police had left, the magician thrust a pair of old red Wellington Boots into Moretaine's hands and shooed him away. Not very polite, thought Moretaine, but poor old magician's clearly thrown off balance by the crass people who tried to remove his modest possessions.

"Take these red wellingtons," said the magician tightly, "and remember, they are to be worn but once - at the school race tomorrow" and left for his small retiring room.

Next day, Moretaine arrived at 8pm at the course, to put in some early practice. It had rained overnight and the ground was muddy. Thank goodness I have the old red wellies, he thought, and slipped them on. He lined himself up to practice the start, and shouted 'bang!" as the starter. The boots promptly bounded up into the air taking Moretaine with them, and came down upright, yards in front of the line. Moretaine looked at the boots with new respect. The magician wasn't so mad after all. Moretaine tried again, "Bang!" and again he was propelled upwards. "Yes," he shouted, and saw in a flash that the Magician like 'Onwards' were on his side and that both wanted him to win, him! - the most cross-eyed boy on the block!

As they waited, the crowds of proud parents were now arriving in small numbers and looked on with trepidation at their nervous offspring, fidgeting on the tracks. The mothers longed for cups of tea the men for pints of beer. Both wanted it all over, without let or hindrance. 'Onwards' stood by his charges, pistol in hand.

"Don't you think," whispered Moretaine to 'Onwards', "people might laugh at anyone who runs a race in red wellington boots?"

"They'd better," growled 'Onwards, "if they know what is good for them!"

'Onwards' was never taken in by the minor jealousies , the schoolboy envies and silly parental ambitions at all such events. When the crowd had reached its permitted maximum, some onlookers began pointing at Moretaine and laughing derisively at 'the squinty boy in red wellington boots.' But ' Onwards' and Moretaine had worked out a simple plan to deal with these proud, disdainful ones. 'Onwards' and his charge remained aloof, indifferent, paring their finger nails. 'Cool' was simply not in it. Moretaine had detected a winning tendency from somewhere in their mutual bonded, comportment. 'Onwards' had gauged it right on the head again.

"Bang!" went the starter's gun. And the boots, Moretaine still inside, bounded off to an amazing start. He was ahead of the field at the first bounce. The obstacles of the race had been laid out with devilish precision and cunning, there was the holly bush hedge, its prickles at the ready, down to its last protected robin hood nests, the builder's planks with splinters, for crossing the pond, - insidious defences - a tumble-down dovecote full of weasels, a puzzled bull swinging its horns and testicles, a Danish Camp run by Taffs, a stile without a sign, a deep river with treacherous currents, all of which Marsden Moretaine did not run into, but bounded over. The other racers were soon tangled up the nets and webs of outrageous fortune. When it came to the river, Moretaine, as planned, changed tactics. He dived in and darted along the river-bed like a rainbow trout, and then bounded out, dripping with water, over the Holly tree into the open, broad sunlit uplands, straight into a line of washing, but sped into the final turn trailing clouds of shirts and socks as he came, but Moretaine's trusty wellies were now dragging along, collecting more disgusting mud, and slowed him to a halt. When he tried to start with a 'bang!' the Wellies gunned like a broken down internal combustion engine and didn't move. The raucous opponents saw bloody Moretaine was in the dire mire and rushed to take advantage of it.

"Onwards!" yelled Onwards,' his final instruction! "Forget your reds! You're on your own feet now! Now Mortaine, do something great for all the cross-eyed people in the world and do it all by yourself!" At once Moretaine realized what he had to do. "Do it!" urged 'Onwards' tremendously again.

Moretaine kicked off his wellies and hurled himself forward although he saw half a dozen finishing lines, running in all directions, he decided to tackle all obstacles in his bare feet at the same time. He followed 'Onwards''s voice above the cacophony of the crowds of prejudiced progenitors, then without warning, slipped and slid on the last slope for a long way and ended up face down in the slough.

"Yes," he thought, "this is the real threat to health and sanity - to let down kindly Magicians, to fail top teachers, to stick in the mud at the National Junior Schools' Obstacle Championship Race, a disappointment for all wall-eyed people, low and high, everywhere.'

However the Magician, now joined 'Onwards' in person and yelled encouragement into Moretaine's dirty ears! Their distant yells reached Moretaine's fatigued brain - but so did the jeers of his peers.

"Hell!" he said almost in tears to 'Onwards', "they're still making fun of me."

"No, they are not Moretaine! Can't you hear the hush that has fallen all over the land?! Can't you see, they are flummoxed as hell.

Look, your big toe is over the line and you have won," shouted 'Onwards,' proudly, so all could hear, "that mediocre mob have turned their coats and are making a hero outta you. Wait till this gets out to the general public, think of all the bug-eyed people in the world - well, you are their hero, a sight for sore eyes for endless races to come! Yes, Marsden Moretaine, Onwards!" and the onlookers did not bar Moretaine's paths to glory. With their useless false cheers still echoing to the skies, Moretaine faced up to the fact that he had actually won the National Junior Championship Obstacle Course silver cup in his tenth year to heaven, with or without praise or calumny. Nobody asked why the trophy in the glass case in the School Hall stood next to a pair of muddied red wellington boots, all surmounted by a huge single ophthalmic eye staring straight ahead, in perfect focus, forever. Moretaine's therapeutic racecourse was instantly established as the foremost cure for defective vision, and many saw uni-focal points beyond belief for the very first time.

"All part of the miracle," said 'Onwards' casually picking his nose. 'You can now see, no doubt,' he continued with a toss of the soiled handkerchief, "that it's as simple as that."

How Suleiman the Squirrel Learned to Jump

Suleiman the Squirrel stood on the end of the branch of a spreading old oak tree, talking angrily to himself. Suleiman's main problem was that he could never learn to jump properly. His Dad and Mum had tried to teach him but had given up in exasperation, "we have given birth to an idiot!" his father declared and Mum went into one of her diatribes about diabetes. Suleiman had heard it all before. And they, him, for they spied on him from the next tree branch, tooth and nail. How Mum hated her son's moans about 'lack of nuts in the home,' "consider the starving hords of Africa," she had yelled at him, "and be grateful for what you've got!" 'She would say that, wouldn't she?' Suleiman called out to himself about her, "she's not out there in the poorly drained pathways of famished townships where they defecate into Littlewood's plastic bags and throw them into the streams of mud and excrement running past the door. Oh, no!" he now addressed the Nimbus clouds forming above, "she's not on her hands and knees picking out grains, eating elephant dung. Yes, Mum, Dad, I know about the starving masses of the banks of the Oronico too, but, Mum, why do I have to join them? I mean, I've read the dailies on poverty, hearkened to the radio bulletins on hunger, watched the lack of food debates in the House of Commons, why don't you at least give me some allowance for being attentive, well read, informed, and sorry about the lack of grains ? I would have thought that was worth a nut or two. Yet you still pretend I don't know anything about the skinny outcast tribes of the Congo or the walking skeletons of their internecine civil conflicts. Of course I know," he yelled into the foliage where he thought his parents were listening, "why pretend I don't? All I want is a nut or two to see me through when I feel peckish." Suleiman's tail drooped, always a sign of deep chagrin.

He could always see the nuts and acorns, but try as he might, he always hesitated at the crucial jump-off point and would invariably end up flat on his nose in the ground. Today was no different. In his hopes for breakfast, he had leapt off the branch, and down he went and landed with a with a thump, and lay there like a dessicated plank. But thanks again, he had just missed Magdalena, his Mum's au pair, who jumped back in fright.

"I told you never to do that again," she said, almost ready to box his ears, "next time, whistle or fart or something." Tears gathered in Suleiman's eyes. "To do that to you! Never! And these are tears of frustration," he declared, "the most unkindest cut of all!"

"Your bloody old Mum and Dad, they'll never give up persecuting you. "

"Tell me about it."

"You're the fall guy every time."

"You don't have to spell it out, like 'the starving hords' of Stockholm, and all that crap. I've got nag-bag Mum *and* barking out loud mad Dad to contend with, I've got the mental bruises to prove it. It's just that before I jump at even the closest of acorns, my courage sort of all shrivels up, my stomach contracts, and I know I can't make it, like just now. I seem to live my life among penumbras, undetermined precipices and spectral famines."

"You are far too distraught," said Magdalena "and I'm just as fed up with hearing you land with a thump on the ground. Now, above all other domestic considerations, I am determined to finally get you off my chest. I've cracked the nut – speaking metaphorically, of course."

"So metaphorically what?" Suleiman asked ungraciously.

"I've been watching you jumping with your Dad."

"That dreadful spectacle of total failure," exclaimed Suleiman, hiding his eyes in shame.

"A hoot a minute, I agree! Flat as a pancake every drop!"

"You must be a prat, a twat, a rat to watch that."

"Don't you dare use that language to me! Or it'll be straight to your Mum."

"No, I was only joking, honest."

"I've been secretly filming your Dad," said Magdalena, "so pay attention, you stunted little trembler, "I have all his jumps on the tablet here. There are certain techniques he leaves out which he never tells you. I have it all on my tablet."

She switched on. Suleiman watched in envious silence. He saw his Dad foraging for nuts and acorns among the boughs with the most brilliant, skilful hops, kicks and jumps. In no time, he had denuded a dozen trees of their fruit. Mounds of nuts and acorns lay ready for removal. Mum stashed them all away in a trice in the undergrowth.

"Well, what did you notice?" asked Magdalena, holding up the tablet.

"Do not probe me please, I am my own man."

"Not yet, buster! Now bend a ear. I have here a series of your Dad's longest jumps, now watch this one, the farthest of the lot."

"God, Dad's good," Suleiman had the last bit of character to admit, "the shite!"

"I'll re-run that. Now three seconds before he jumps, and this time – watch his head!"

Suleiman followed Magdalena's key instructions to the letter 'T'. He suddenly sat bolt upright. "Re-run!" he shouted again and again. Then he sang out, "the bastards, their dastardly secret is secret no more. I have it!" Listen!" he brayed at the universe. "The formula? "- 'Don't look right, don't look left, look straight ahead – raise your head, point your nose," he added in a sort of revelation, "and just jump!"

"The way and the life!" chimed in Magdalena triumphantly, hoping at last that she had rid herself of her pea-brained, barely sexual hanger on.

Suleiman chanted the silly mantra again, "Don't look left. Don't look right. Look straight ahead - raise your head, point your nose, and just - jump!" sang Suleiman to the oaks and orchards of the world, enthralled - "just do it!"

"Now back to your branch, and rock'n roll again!""

Suleiman scampered up the old acorn tree, stood right at the very end of a swaying branch, poised like a swimmer of the skies, gave one proud look around, nose up, head high, and gave the most confident leap he had ever made in his life! He landed like a veteran lands where he has exactly aimed for, on his fluffy four legs in an upright posture with a handful of nuts he had grabbed on the way down, to prove he had really been there.

Just at that moment, they heard the familiar sarcastic voice of Dad from the next tree burst out in involuntary surprise, "well, bless my soul, Mum, if I didn't just see our idiot boy make a bit of a real dive. What a turn up in the ranks!"

"Huh!" Mum grunted sardonically, "don't believe a word he says," and went into an endless Phillipic about her blossoming varicose veins and their variegated treatment.

But it was Suleiman, as he prepared for his next move, who had the last word:

"One step for a squirrel but a giant leap for squirrel kind!"

These famous words went down in history and Suleiman never failed again.

Fabula Meets the Fair Folk of Iffland

It had been a stormy night and Fabula was strolling through the garden looking at all the damage the savage winds had done. Her Mum had gone shopping, leaving the mess to her, as usual. Bits of branch and torn leaves littered the lawn. Some of the borders were flattened, the petals of the lupins, delphiniums, the larkspurs and the roses were spread all over the ground. A huge branch from the old oak lay right across Mum's new border. 'Well, she can't blame that on me,'' thought Fabula, 'serves her right!" She remembered her Mum's utterly selfish words, 'someone has to do it,' each flower being grudgingly planted with a meaningful look at her. But why should I, thought Fabula, run around mowing lawns and watering the Cosmos when all the thanks I get is a half a dozen snarls, insults, and threats to rub my nose in the dirt. 'No gardening for me, definitely not.'

She suddenly heard a tap, tap, tapping, like a wood-pecker at work. She stopped. A chorus of little distressed voices came to her ears. It seemed to be coming from coming under the fallen branch. She grasped it and with all her strength, dragged it to one side. She stepped back in surprise at what she saw. Out of the piles of twigs and foliage, brushing off his clothes, emerged a little figure. He wore ordinary gardener's garb and his voice was strained and squeaky, as if it needed oil.

"Free! Free at last," the little manikin cried out. His relief was evident even from high up.

Fabula Meets the Fair Folk of Iffland

Fabula stared open-mouthed, "I can't believe this," she stuttered.

"Fabula, you are my saviour!"

"But who are you?"

"I am a denizen of the flower beds."

"What's a 'denizen'?"

"A guy, a chap, a being. I am from Iffland, representative of the people of the flowers, woods and trees."

"The Fair Folk do not exist, my Mum said so."

"Well, well," said the figure, "my name is Martingale and, as such I exist alright. But does she? Does she exist? Your Mum?"

"Yes, of course she does," said Fabula,' for better or worse."

"Why?"

"Because she's my mother," replied Fabula a little helplessly.

"That's a poor excuse for being in a state of maternity, if you ask me."

"I didn't ask to be born either."

"Not a single human ever did," said Martingale, "but we Fair Folk do, frequently."

"What are you then?"

"We are the spirits of the green places of the planet, the tribe of Iffland, of the Fair Folk. Why, the universe teems with us, the healthy and raw in nature, the untouched, thriving, not the sly and nasty like you humans. Here is my little domain. This patch of green. Your Mum is often in our lives, she loves us as her own, mostly by accident, and cares for us just like her buddleias, although she doesn't really realize how weedy buddleias are. Never mind. She's good for a bucket of water from time to time." He looked around. "Some of my airy fellow entities are here, too, recovering from the terrible battering last night."

"That's a lot of words for something that is not there," observed Fabula, "I think you're letting your imagination run away with you,"

"Then let me introduce them to you, as they shake off the leaves and the detritus of the dark rustling hours."

Martingale beckoned to the opening below the branch which Fabula had just removed. Martingale named the figures as they emerged: "Look, there goes the spirit of the buttercups, note the yellow costume;" a little figure bowed hastily and disappeared into the hazel rods; "there, the daisies, see the white caps and pale complexion; there, the mother of all lupins, in her spotted skirts, the larkspurs with their hooked heels, there go the spirits of the gorse, blown here by the wind, the laburnums, the delphiniums, note in blue, without those silly peaked caps, only honest working leprechauns here, in corduroy and miners' lamps, and that's no joke." The little figures scuttled off into the undergrowth, waving to Fabula and Martingale as they went.

"And we've got a bog sprite too, don't you worry, to balance things out. See, in the compost heap there, the Spirit of Ugh himself, look, he's just climbing out of his slush pile."

A sinister figure in a long slimy cloak wriggled out of the dung and jumped down. Dangerously, he was munching a spray of deadly nightshade - which seemed to make no difference to his health. He sloped off without a word into the cloaca close to the river nearby.

"Now do you believe me?"

"Well, sort of."

"What nebula were you born in! Then watch this!"

He yelled out some incoherent, esoteric, gibberish in all directions. At once the whole garden came alive and was invaded by the stirring shades and embodied spirits of the woods, hundreds of them, representing everything green that grew, all quite cheerful in their working clothes and instantly identifiable by their herbal auras. As if to a plan, they set to with a will and began to tidy up the storm damage, clearing the borders so the flowers again stood proud, erect and spreading, the lawns suddenly unscored, shining and level as before; even the Spirit of Ugh made an effort and smoothed down his noisome pile so it was less conspicuous; then, above them all, on the marge of the woods, above the trees, loomed a gigantic over-spreading figure clothed in the huge lapping leaves of the sycamore and oak, yes! – the famous Green Man himself, Father Protector of the Forests, and the name of a thousand pubs all over the land. Only his gleaming eyes could be seen in the leaf-dominated face. He had a caduceus sort of staff in his hand and he directed operations with merciless precision. All obeyed him with more than just alacrity.

"You see, he's the boss, and they all know it. He's ready now! Watch!"

The Green Man, Father Protector and Director of the woody sprites, now raised his staff. In a twinkle, everyone had vanished, green resorted to green, not a bud remained unturned, not a petal without its dam, not even a fly buzzed over the Ugh's foul midden. At the same time, at the arse end of the vision, a car appeared driving too fast up the drive and pulled up with a screech and a crunch. Out clambered Mum, dragging her shopping bags. The Green Man waved farewell to Fabula, he had had enough of these foul, storm-tossed, thankless humans, and faded into the thick, green-heart wood-mist with his myriad, silent minions.

Fabula's Mum paused and stared, eyes wide, mouth open. What was this greensward which greeted her? Her work of yesterday somehow restored to its original perfect condition. Hers. Once again highly kempt, prim and trimmed, the borders newly intact, the lawn immaculate as shit, not a leaf out of place, as pristine as if there had been no storm at all, not even a coy eddy or two in the outback.

"My goodness, Fabula..." she glowered at her daughter in disbelief, "you've made it all a bit weird, haven't you?!" She frowned suspiciously, "you didn't do this all by yourself, did you?"

Fabula, seeing her mother, the boss, was puzzled - an ominous state for her, usually presaging some kind of destruction - so now no-longer -'useless' -Fabula decided that lying was not the best policy. Her Mum could tell a lie in a thousand-ton bomb crater.

"No, honestly, Mum, I can't say that I did it all by myself."

"I thought as much. Who helped you then?"

"Why, the Fair Folk of the Forest, and the Green Man too!"

Mum sighed – another adolescent fantasy! She looked carefully at the many calculated, expressions flitting across Fabula's face, and gave up. What did it matter? The deed was done. The shopping spree had made her free. And no more bluddy gardening today, thank God! She looked at her daughter again more closely, what a clever horticulturist Fabula would make when she grew up - just like her mother!

Phylomena and Fitzbal in Converse

Phylomena flounced into her bedroom. How dare her Mum nag her again over the self-raising flour. It wasn't her, Phylomena , who had spilled it, it was the flour itself which had sent itself toppling off the table onto the floor. Anybody could see that. Her Mum was such a pest. "It isn't the flour, it's the principle!" she had said out loud, for all to hear.

Phylomena looked at her friends on the bed, Tony the Tiger, Leo the Leopard, Ali the Gator, Katty the Kat. She grabbed her lovely raggedy talking 'Fitzbal' Bear, her oldest friend from ages ago, and pulled the ring on the cord from the back. "I'm glad we're friends," came a faint mechanical voice. "Oh, come on," said Phylomena. She put in a new battery, and pulled the ring again. This time the voice was loud and clear, "I'm glad we're friends!" "That's better, Fitzbal! I was just saying that Mum is getting to be just an old nag bag, especially in the kitchen. What can I do?"

"Don't take it so tragically," said Fitzbal quietly, "It's just her change of life."

"Then why doesn't she tell me about it. Does she think I'm a child or what? I know about these things. I use my ears. Yes, She should confide in me."

"Perhaps she just doesn't want to worry you."

"Why does she always treat me as if I was blind, deaf and dumb,

Fitzbal ? I get more respect from you than ever from her, and she's supposed to be grown up. I've seen all her problems, heard them all, felt them all, so 'don't condescend', I told her last night, "just be yourself."

"Well," said Fitzbal, he knew the best way to get his friend Phylomena out of her vile mood was to distract her. He changed the subject to something much more intriguing.

"Where do you go when you sleep?" he asked.

Phylomena calmed down at once. "What do you mean, Fitzbal ?"

"Where?"

"I don't 'where' at all, I'm just a shape, an outline if you wish, inclined on a bed."

"How can you know where you go if you're sleep?"

"Well... I suppose I don't..."

"...ask them," said Fitzbal, pointing at Phylomena's friends on the bed.

"Alright. I like this game."

"It's not a game," said Ali the Gator sitting up.

"Where do you go then?" she asked him, but before he could reply there was a sudden loud crackle and whizzle, and Ali the Gator was gone.

"Help," said Phylomena , quite taken aback.

"Ask Tony the Tiger, Katty the Kat and Leo the Leopard then."

But before she had even started to ask, there were more crackles and whizzles - three times! And then Tony, Katty and Leo were gone.

"Come back. You're my friends. I'll feed you!" she cried. But it was too late. "Don't leave me, Fitzbal ? That's an order!" she added. She was still in charge.

"Don't worry, I'm here for the duration," Fitzbal assured her - 'the bitch!'

Again abrupt crackles and whizzles, and Tony re-appeared on the bed, then Katty, Leo and Ali. They didn't seem afraid, just a bit sleepy and rubbed their eyes. Then, whizzle and crackle, they were gone again and then back, and gone again, all higgledy-piggledy, like a bunch fleas all jumping from fluff to fluff in a warm pillow case.

"Stop, stop!" cried Phylomena , "what's happening?"

"They're showing you where they go when you're asleep,"

"What?"

"Why do you think I'm still here?"

"Why?"

"Because you're awake. When you're asleep, I whizz away to a girl or boy who have also just woken up. They have to have their friends by their sides too. Then when they fall asleep again, the Leo's and the Ali's from all over the world, return to their homes, like I return to you here, so you're never alone either."

Phylomena looked accusingly at him. "You said that on purpose, didn't you, to distract my attention so I wouldn't be angry any more with Mum. "Well..." she was surprised at the attack of remorse which suddenly fell on her like a sack of potatoes, "you're right, I was wrong! Self-raising flower is a paltry thing to quarrel over. I shall wait for a more momentous occasion. I shall say 'I'm sorry' to Mum when she comes home, and tell her that if she doesn't want to talk about her change of life, it's perfectly alright with me and I'll clear up all the flour. And when she says suspiciously, "Why this sea-change?" as she will, I shall just say 'crackle and whizzle', dear Mum, because I want to be here for you when you're in bed, like Fitzbal and all my friends even when you're asleep! And then I'll completely throw her by giving her give her a great big hug. And what'll she say? Listen."

She tugged on the ring on Fitzbal's back, "I'm glad we're friends..."

"...and so am I!" responded Fitzbal with a real man-made chuckle.

131

The Lopsided Corporal of Grenadiers

Sylvanus, the old carpenter, lived at Pinewood House in the centre of town. As Sylvanus grew more and more skilled in the art of carving in wood, he switched from plain commodes and officers's travelling trunks, to swags of fruit in holy chapels and the escritoires of Louis Quinze. This was the point where he began to model first, then carve in wood, amazing likenesses of the human figures, of all sizes, nations, faiths and sexes. The shelves of his shop were stacked with dolls and figurines; duchesses and cooks, princes and footpads, riders to the hunt, and followers on foot, beetle-browed academics, ten-year old chimney sweeps, hundred-year-old marchionesses, nimble 110-year old hermits, exceptionally young members of the Fair Folk tribe, he covered the whole spectrum of humanity, and beyond, from erection to resurrection – as they say - all shapefully nude or exquisitely costumed. He specialized in working the almost invisible minutiae of the most delicate veins just below the epiglottal superficies in the abdominal region, as well as the equally important outer casing of man, vestments that glittered with silver leaf, gold braid and splendid 23 carrot buttons, coat-hanger masterpieces. He soon became famous in every nook and cranny of this cash-register called 'world'; and fashionable? Man! - everyone wanted a doll from his shop. He adapted like the unchanging chameleon - people loved war, so he became a specialist in toy soldiers; grenadiers holding their bombs, light infantry wielding their bayonets, artillery men, down to the last cannon, even to the time fuses, all set, and the blood clutter of the enemy over the caissons done brilliant. He loved his work, people loved his work. Sylvanus prospered. But one day when he was working at his bench, he noticed his bones creaked a bit, especially the finger joints, where he developed ominous lumps. Arthritis was it? Rheumatic bumps? Or just the rot of the ages? Slowly he came to the realization that his fingers were beginning to stiffen up on a permanent basis. In a few months he could wield a chisel no longer, nor hold the humble nail, nor utilize the essential hammer, the carpenter's universal friend. He often dropped his drills and screwdrivers from numbed hands, his wooden replicas distorted and horrible, lacking all expertise. He sometimes wept as he beheld his precious once-familiar instruments lying useless on the work bench, and sobbed bitterly at the horrid little still-births he was seemingly alone capable of producing. But people still wanted his work, hideous or not, if they had his signature. Collectors came from far and wide to snap up his remaining pieces, however wretched, until at last, there was only one piece left, a Beefeater, the popular name for the personal royal body-guard at the grim Tower of London, of the Tudor line, who defended the Tower and all its wonderful gems of purest ray serene, its gleaming coronets, against all comers, even pretty poor ones. These meat-eating royal Guardians were specially selected from the most fashionable regiments because there was no class bias at the front.

Sad to relate, the Doll Mender had become the Doll Breaker. He abruptly stopped working on the last sprawling Beefeater in mid-paralysis. He had been trying to re-create it in Leonardo's image of divine human perfection, the one he had famously drawn in a squared circle in his notebook. But even this last dream of one hundred-per-cent harmony, the golden mean of Arcadia, dribbled away. His inspiration lay at last inert on the jaques floor. He could not now remove even the thinnest veneer from a simple door panel. Even his abortions ceased - an unachievable art had been born. He made his final farewell to his workbench amid floods of tears, tearing sobs and uncontrollable hiccoughs. He abandoned the solitary Beefeater, the last of the Grenadier Corporals, on his shelf, leaning backwards, its skinny legs spread out before him, its trunk thin as a bean pole, slumped sideways, his head nearly hanging off, misshapen, unnatural, unfamiliar and therefore someone rejected by the healthier members of the community; his costume a rusty jingle-jangle-jungle of second-hand tin and aluminium. That did it. No one wanted to look at the last, new leper- Corporal, 'the lopsided soldier,' the Grenadier casualty, let alone buy him. The shop became as derelict as a deserted hospital barrack square on an icy Winter's night.

Sylvanus was as broke, broken and famished as his last Grenadier. He cruised his cellars and attics in search of mice and even rat fodder. He was being driven mad by thoughts of nibbles. One day, he groped forward and his hand hit the bread bin. It tumbled to the floor, and there behind where it had lain for so long, stood exposed to the light of day, a piece of traditional English nutritional fare, a Hovis crust, covered with green mold, perhaps, but intact as shit. It had been lurking behind the bin. He immediately hurried over to his seemingly anaesthetized comrade, revived him with the last drop of Napoleon brandy in Pinewood, tore the bread in half before the suffering Corporal's eyes, his very eyes, and offered him the last morsel, the guy was getting thinner by the minute, fast fading away and up in smoke. The Grenadier's eyes widened in gratitude. His mouth gasped. Hunger incarnate garbled his words but there was no doubt that the old soldier's deepest thanks lay deep among them. Sylvanus! What a mate! What a comradely offer! Quite stunning! The Corporal, momentarily refreshed by hope which eternally clings to the human breast, - fuckin' imposter!- staggered to his weedy feet and gave a slow but snappy regimental salute. What a mucker was this Sylvanus to have in a tight corner, pantry or kitchen. But the gallant old Corporal was moved so profoundly by the humanity of the gesture, by its sheer virtuosity, that he was, out of simple politeness and thankfulness, constrained to decline the health-giving wheaten offer with uplifted hand.

"No mate of mine goes starving if there's one bit of crust left,' declared the Grenadier Corporal, and returned the portion of green slice into the very giving hands of the great-spirited Sylvanus. Comrades-in-arms indeed! Sharers of the Hovis loaf to the bitter end - even if it wasn't shared, in death, it remained undivided! The old Doll Mender collapsed, weeping at the life-and-death affirming rejection, then himself lapsed into what appeared to be a final dog-like coma. The blessed Grenadier peeked at his mate's now fading physog. No, not a coma, just a temporary blackout due to sheer disappointment, not only at his rotting fingers no doubt, but also at the tragic refusal of the generosity of a slice of ambrosial green anglian Hovis. Sylvanus knew it was the most noble gesture he had ever seen, but because, with Sylvanus acting as commanding officer, neither could the ranking Corporal or Sylvanus himself, propose the royal toast - not a drop of bloody hooch in the house, - 'The Queen, god bless her!' – I think, he thought, as, overcome by thunderous stomach growls, Sylvanus slowly slid to the floor, taking the grenadier with him. How he still clung onto his heavy-breathing guide and mentor. They lay together, the hungry faithful duo of the times, the loyal Beefeater above, lopsided on the shelf, and the divinely gifted woodcarver, the Doll Mender, the still famous Sylvanus, spread-eagled, emaciated as shit, sad to tell, again, on the floor in his bare bones. What a sorry pass, twice, was there!

Out of the universal chamber of Fortune herself, there came a tap, tap tapping at the shop door. A face peered through the dusty panes. It was the Corporation dust-cart Receiver, checking the rubbish to make sure it was in order, like not protruding one inch above the plastic lid or clotted with immigrant fluid. But the Doll

Mender's bin was filled to overflowing only with cast offs, none of any nutritional value. It was as if the Householder had thrown his last pathetic possessions away in one last desperate appeal for help. 'No peelings, no feelings, no eats, no sweets, no breath, just death!' The Dust Man, or Receiver of Ordure, to give him his full title, fair play, pushed the door open. Poor old Sylvanus hadn't even had the strength to turn the key in the lock.

The Ordure Receiver was confronted by one of the saddest spectacles of his corporative experience – one of his favourite customers down and out in full sight, and the last doll, which he did not covet, he admitted quite frankly, making a sad spectacle on the shelf above, lying terribly lop-sided. Between them lay a slice of green brown bread, in two portions, 'Hovis' by name. The Dustman sized up the little tragedy in a trice. He hurried out to his cart. He had just done the prosperous posh crescents, gardens and mews, and had plenty of top goodies which could be liberated for his old skin and bone customer and his comrade. He grabbed a box of Welsh cakes, a peasantry boon for the true blues, a jar of caviar, a loaf of French bread, still warm from the oven, and dashed back. In a second, old Sylvanus was soon hunched over the most delicious feast he had ever had in his life. The Beefeater, thin no longer, looked down beaming, stuffing his gob, chuffed to be once again on the job, doing nothing, and stealing other people's grub.

"You wait," said the Dustman to the Beefeater, "I've got just the thing for you!"

He hurried out and was back at once, carrying a huge T bone steak on a paper plate. "Beef a la mode!" he said triumphantly, "now sit on the counter with your mate, Sylvanus here, with my timing watch ready, steady, go! "

In a second, that Beefeater had beaten all records for beef eating. The Tower would be proud of him again! His back straightened, his figure filled out, his chin tucked in, his pace became martial again. The Dustman then brought in the cream of the cream, a thrice-whipped almond ice-cream magnum bar from the city of Milan! They all sat at the counter now, chomping and chuckling and sighing and biting and farting and burping, a veritable heaven of sound ironically made out of a real hell of body noises, a symphony out of gutsy discords - the Beefeater beaming, the Doll Mender mending, the dust man, or Ordure Receiver, re-dispensing salient bits of flesh, a picture of the harmony and fraternity that frail humanity can attain to! - "So," Sylvanus declared to the new brotherhood, repeating what his dear old Mam had often whispered into his ear, 'be not forgetful to entertain strangers, for thereby some have entertained angels unawares!' - Sylvanus, urged on by the Corporal Grendier at his best, swallowed a jar of caviar and pointed straight at the Dustman, their best friend the Receiver, an 'angel unawares!'! How the Grenadier and Sylvanus cheered him on. The Ordure Receiver was in his seventh heaven to be a comrade in such distinguished company was a royal honour in itself, up to the standard of The Times, and Guardian too! Sylvanus made the final toast - 'Salut, mes braves! '- as Louis Quinze used to say! 'And bon appétit!'

Count Hemlock, Countess Manexora, and Princess Miriama

The little Princess called Miriama lay on the stone floor of her room - more of a prison cell than a room, really. She had on a ragged night gown and her feet were bare. Her fingers were blue and she was shivering. She was locked in the highest chamber of the Dark Tower, wreathed, as it was, from top to toe in thick, clustrous ivy, especially of the poisonous kind, and which never let in any of the essential warm sunlight of life. Although she was called 'princess,' she wasn't a direct line descendent, just a cadet branch claimant. Her father was a bastard on top of this. Before and after he disappeared, the bend sinister had always featured prominently in his coat of arms, but like Rhett, he didn't give a damn. King Karian as he called himself, twentieth of the line, and his 'Princes Miriama' as he was constrained to call her, the disobedient, mulish little bitch of a rebellious teenager! Jesus, women! He'd teach her a lesson. But the lesson never materialized and her great aunt, Manexora, as toxic a harpy as you'd ever wish to meet, was next in line - so she said - another 'royal' bloody liar. King Kariad felt he had not remonstrated enough with her. If only Miriama had kept her mouth shut and had not called her randy aunty 'a harlot of the first water, given to unnatural practices', and put pictures abroad, and in Court in particular, of her aunty, bent over, with a huge donkey, a straw hat over his ears, doing the honours. Even though Manexora swore the pictures had been re-touched and air brushed in the vital areas, the pictures became a collectors' item. The scandal died down but Miriama had made a deadly enemy. "If only you had kept your mouth shut, you self-indulgent hot-head, you are just as randy as her, only you keep your hand inside your nickers. That's the only excuse you've got, you two-faced wanker" Those proved to be the royal father's final admonition to his beloved daughter.

Every night, at six o'clock, after cleaning the shoes, polishing the silver, washing up her aunty's undies, she was dismissed to her 'room.' But not to rest or to sleep. There were always jobs to be done before bed - the 'bed' being a cot, really, with three planks and an old army horse-hair blanket - always more toil waiting, ingeniously nasty stuff, invented by her hag of an aunt. And she had to finish the tasks, however impossible it seemed, by dawn. Tonight, she saw one corner was filled to the ceiling with a mountainous pile of goose feathers, the very feathers she had toiled to pluck the night before. Now she had to fill two dozen bolsters by first light and each feather had to be put in carefully, one by one. The pillows were for ambitious, greedy, faddist, Manexora, who could only sleep on the softest of downs, eat the most delicate of food – cooked haute cuisine especially by her niece - three times a day – finicky bad cat! Manexora would know immediately if just one feather had been inserted too hastily or one potato was over-mashed - in which case, Princess Miriama would have to do a re-count or a re-cook of the offending spud, whichever the case.

The Castle and the Dark Tower had belonged to her father, King Kariad, not the most rightful monarch but the most insistent. One day from this very chamber, he had observed in the distance his lands and farmsteads , crops and orchards, being consumed by fire , the wheat fields torched, the fishponds ransacked, by his brother-in-law, Count Hemlock, the warped aunty's husband and consort. The King had rallied his retainers and had charged through the devastated farms and fields after his enemy. He disappeared at the head of his troops into the smoke of war, and had never re-appeared. But Count Hemlock, her uncle-in-law, did, and with who? - side by side with Countess Manexora, Manexora who turned out to be far more savage and blood-thirsty than her lousy husband. She plunged Princess Miriama into the lofty cell, and closed every entrance to it, whereas her father had always kept every door open, however fraudulent his claim to the throne. Now the whole grim place was locked and barred and the keeper of the keys, the only one, was Countess Manexora with her fiend-like grin and flailing mace.

The icy wind moaned into the room making the cold flags even colder. Miriama stood in the moonlight streaming in from the one shutterless window. She sobbed, looking up at the herculean dawn, down task.

"I can't do this. I can't. Daddy!" she blurted out, "save me, save my body and my sanity. I can't go on. You were so accurate in your assessment of Manexora and her nasty Count Hemlock . I apologise for my flawed adolescent judgements. Honest, Dad. When are you coming home? The rice pudding is in the oven and the mead warming by the fire. I love you. I will never forget you. I will never give up fighting for your many rights, whatever the additions, corrections, and erasures to the certificates - especially mine, my rights, I mean..."

The wind died down and she heard an odd flap-flapping from the ivy. Suddenly a shadow parked itself at the window. She steeled herself and approached. It was, yes, a Gray Owl and a huge one. His eyes were big as saucers and shone like gig lamps. The Gray Owl seemed to stare straight through her. In his claws he had a bleeding, crushed little corpse, an unfortunate mole, who had crossed his path in his nocturnal slaughter grid-patterns.

He seemed passive enough. His eyes flickered, but not in hostility. 'But he is alone,' she thought, 'even if he is big and his eyes are bright as flame, they are still somehow very comforting. Yes, look for the man within,' and her fears eased at once. 'Perhaps he's looking for a friend and ally too.' Then his gaze settled on little Miriama and at once she saw his eyes were full of the unwatered milk of human kindness, very unusual for a predatory creature with talons, however illusory his acts of compassion. Instinctively for a girl, Miriama reached out to him. Without let, hindrance, or question, he released the little bleeder in his claws, his gift, his offer for friendship. Miriama, never squeamish at events such as these, delicately picked it up by the tail and hurled it out of the window! Gray Owl blinked once and enfolded her in his cosy, welcoming, blood-splattered wings.

"Come in out of the cold, Old Gray Owl," she said, a little tentatively.

"'Wise' Old Gray Owl, if you please," he replied, blinking in a greenish kind of way.

"Of course, that was what I meant, Mr Wise Old Gray Owl."

"Now I come to think of it, just Gray Owl is OK," he replied.

She felt her spirits lift at once at this little act of generosity and the wicked pile of feathers suddenly looked much less daunting.

"Where do you live, Gray Owl?"

"I usually live in the ivy, I have a very comfortable billet there, and it's quite safe. But ever since your nasty aunty Manexora closed up the tower and plunged you into durance vile, I haven't been able to sleep. And when I hear you weeping every night, I begin to weep too. This had got to stop, or we'll both end up known as just a pair of misery-guts, black-eyed melancholics, discontented with our lot."

"Very perspicacious, Wise Owl. It's my pernicious aunty Manexora, she is at the root of every degenerate and barbaric code of behaviour."

"Been there," said Gray Owl, "got the scarf. I've been watching that old harpy from my ivy bower for years. I know her vicious ways and means. Leave her to me. And don't worry about your Dad. If there's one man I've ever known in my sideways life who never gave up, it was your dear, strong King Kariad, although his claim is very dicey indeed. But who cares, he's our man, he is after all, so distingue. Wait and watch, be patient, above all, be delighted whatever the foul sights, vile vanities and ego shite-hawks you encounter from time to time, along the broad and easy highways of the Dark Side!"

What perceptive, comforting words! Princess Miriama glowed. Yes, she was sure, she had found a true friend and ally, in spite of the recently employed claws.

"Gray Owl looked at the monstrous, unnecessary pile of feathers. "What a thankless task!" he said, "but leave that to me, too. My friends of the ubiquitous flocks of the world, and I know all about feathers, after all, that's what we're mostly made of, in the final analysis, I mean."

The little Princess gave a little laugh, a tinkle at first, then like a cracked bell.

"I'd like to hear much more of that delightful sound, the first bit," said Wise Owl, laughing with her. "It was not quite genuine, yet not quite dishonest, sort of socially tentative, overdone, don't worry, acceptable at this moment in time. Now, do you like birthday parties?"

"I don't know. I've never had one."

"'Never!?" Not one?" Miriama shook her head. Gray Owl persisted, "not even a single solitary one?"

"Please don't be so persistent. I mean what I say..."

"...and...?"

"My Dad was preparing a special one for me just before Manexora and her loathsome Count Hemlock stepped in with their filthy incendiary matches and poisoned bows and arrows - as if this place was up the Amazon - and set the savannas aflame."

Gray Owl frowned, "We'll have to do something quick about those two descendents of Sodom, and I mean, in a flash!"

He hopped onto the window sill, and opened his wings wide.

"Come on, then, onto my back!" Miriama hesitated.

"Don't worry, safe as houses. You can trust me, and if you can't, you'd be dead by now anyway."

Miriam nodded. The comfort of logic was in his words. She climbed aboard and settled down, clinging to the broadest feathers on his back. This was fun.

"Where are we going?"

"To a birthday party."

"But I haven't got a proper dress," she said sadly, looking down at her rags.

"Leave that to me," he said. "Now hang on, Miriama," he said using her name for the first time. He slowly allowed himself to fall out smoothly into the open illuminated moon-space below. Down the white gigantic air he swooped, zoomed up again, then straight ahead at cruising height and speed. The Dark Tower was soon left far behind, a mere odious memory. It was so soft in Gray Owl's feathers, she shuddered, but this time from pleasure. The world up here was so peaceful, she thought, the only sound was the wind in Gray Owl's wings and the only sight, the puffed up clouds shining mute and stationary in the hemisphere. 'I must be the only floating Princess in the whole bright universe,' she thought and hugged Grey Owl.

"Careful, no shenanigins on the flight deck," he immediately warned.

"I didn't mean anything," Miriama protested.

"Well, I did," said Gray Owl, "so none of those which I just mentioned."

"Have it your way, I suppose, you're boy owl. Look! The moon's so close," she said, "I feel I could reach out and touch it."

"That old Moon," said Gray Owl, "she stares at me from there every live-long night and never says a word. No idea why. I never meant any offense. You'll see more of her on this trip I promise you."

He pointed downwards. Far below, thousands of different coloured sparklets of light twinkled into view

"Look," exclaimed Miriama pointing at the stars, "as thick as meadow of daisies in Spring. What place is this?" she asked, enchanted by the view of islands looming below. "Are they the Kingdoms of the Fair Folk of Iffland ? The Realms of the Mermaids? The Lair of the Leprechauns? Look, I can see the waves blown back all around it, white and black. Yes do you think they will sing to me?!"

"That," said Gray Owl, "is a moot point. But over there is the Island where Birthday Parties Never End! And that's exactly where we're going to, too!"

He went into a deep dive, then pulled up sharply, hovering only a few hundred feet above ground, his flapping wings went 'whap, whap!' like a Vietnam helicopter. Miriama saw they were flying over the tops of the trees and the multi-coloured illuminations came from thousands of candles all placed along the boughs of the magic oaks and other mythological species of trees, like the ash or the holy Thorn of Glastonbury. On the ground stood thousands of candles on hundreds of birthday cakes, all lit up, an exhilarating sight, but one which 'must have cost a fortune,' thought Miriama. 'Anything to keep up with the joneses, I suppose.'

"Why, that island is full of birthday parties," exclaimed Miriam clapping her hands. "Will the cost never end?"

"You must put all thought of expense out of your pretty head, Miriama," said Gray Owl severely, "I told you to leave it to me. I can arrange a loan at five short percent, OK? And the parties never end," added Gray Owl, "at least not on this island and if your repayments are on time, OK?"

"Look," cried Miriama again, "a panda birthday party!"

She looked in awe at the fun, the pandas were dancing in circles with paper hats on their heads, all roly-poly, and when the stopped they curled up into round bundles of wool, and went to the toilet on the spot. The little Princess laughed with delight at their antics. "How normal," she cried, "it's quite a natural thing, after all."

"Well put, Miriama, and very humane too, we've all been caught short sometime. But Pandas," sniffed Gray Owl, "can't really dance, they just roll over like Beethoven, in balls , and balls can't dance, it's well known, they bounce, but they're friendly enough."

"This is so far from those awful memories of pillage and rapine," said Miriama, "don't worry, I know the meanings of those terrible words, my Daddy held up the book of life to me and said I should know the most important thing in it, which is TRUTH. And that includes the dark side, the rape and the repossessions, hobbies of the wicked witches of the West, or is it East, and how it all spills over into greed, ambition, murder and mayhem, being born at all, in fact, like unrestrained lust, defecation, menstruation in public places, copulation in extremis, that sort of thing," she said, getting the simple truth all garbled up, a pity, because her heart was not quite yet in the right place.

"A wise monarch your Dad, something like me," said Gray Owl modestly. "The saddest of things are in that book, but the bestest too, like what we're doing now."

"You are so right, Gray Owl, I love you!" and she kissed him out of sheer, impulsive affection. Gray Owl felt a little urge but suppressed it, glowed a little, and zoomed down again for more views of the same. The pandas did hail and farewell rolls and bouncec of honour as they sped away.

"And those acrobatics were quite genuine too," Miriama couldn't resist defending the pandas. They were so cute.

"Of course, always throw in a bit of the truth with the lies and they'll always believe it. Machiavelli, you know, wise owl of the Renaissance."

"Look," cried Miriam, pointing, "this defies credibility, although I like it."

She pointed at a huge open space on the ground, "look, those kangaroos there are having a terrific party, very athletic, but can you credit it? playing leap-frog! Look, and jumping so far over the back of the next kangaroo, they disappear wheeeeeee - over the rim of night! Outta sight, man!"

Miriama and Wise owl now laughed as one, they were so far into it. The vanishing kangaroos carried on merrily jumping out of one earthly existence into another unknown dimension just for the fun of it, all on the Island where birthday parties never end.

"Those kangaroos are not very bright," commented Gray Owl, "their mental horizon is limited, but, by goodness, they are great for a laugh and are champions of the world in the disappearing fast!"

"Oops!" cried the Princess, as they flew low over the next wood of soaring red pines, some as old as Jesus. Heads began popping up above the forest canopy.

"Help Gray Owl, what is happening?"

"Sorry, my fault. Flew too low that time."

"But all these heads, such expressions of curiosity ...?"

"Just giraffes, curious as kittens they are, just popping up through the foliage to see the goings on. Oops! There we go again. They may be tall but they lack all sense of discretion. But don't worry, they have hides an inch thick and no one can get through to them, including me. My razor-sharp claws are as matchsticks to them.

"But why they don't look up when they're looking down, is beyond me," said Miriama, "they could cause serious accidents."

"Well," replied, Gray Owl, "they don't like people looking down on them, which is fair enough, OK, but please next time," he shouted at the popping up heads, "give us a warning! They're really quite generous souls on the ground," he added, "but sometimes they're a bit of a traffic hazard, you're quite right. Now I'm going to land on that palm-tree for a drop of fermented coco juice and a breather." He fluttered down right onto on a bunch of lovely coconuts.

" First class!" cried the Princess, "we're right on the sea-shore!"

She heard splashing from below accompanied by sounds of satisfied grunts and bellows, and faint snores.

"That can only be a walrus tea-party," said Gray Owl, "you can tell by the sound of blubber on flesh and the snorts of self-satisfaction and blowing bubbles noisily in the air. They're usually inert, lethargic to a 'T', but they have a nasty punch in those flippers, particularly the females, so watch out."

"All you can see is their noses," observed Miriama, laughing,

"Well, wouldn't you, if you were as fat as that. But watch them trying to get out onto the rocks, an epidemic of flabbering obesity before your eyes. They're just waking up," said Gray Owl, "they're so apparently somnolent."

"Why is that?" asked Miriama.

"They sleep in the water,

They sleep on the sand,

They sleep on each other,

They sleep where they stand!" explained gray Owl.

"Yes, I see, but they seem a very friendly lot although they're half blind with fatty tissue. And look, a lot of signposts, all pointing to other parties!"

"We're at the cross-roads of celebration," said, Gray Owl, "see that way, to the Penguin parties, that road , to the Tiger and Bunny Balls, the Monkey Jamborees, just a short walk, but don't get lost there or you'll be chased up the trees all day, cheeky, shitty simians! Simply everyone who is anyone is here or there sometime or other. There are about one thousand parties to choose from, but we can't do many today, we simply don't have the footsteps in the sands of time."

"I can see the Polar Bear party," cried the little Princess in delight, "over there! What are they doing?"

"The Bears are carrying huge cubes of ice covered with snow and mixing them all up in the big tubs, ice cream for all the parties in the land."

"Don't they ever stop?"

"That *is* their birthday party," said Gray Owl, "mixing it all up, so they never stop even for tea, they are far too busy being happy."

Gray Owl bore swiftly to starboard and flew onwards again.

"Look," said Miriam, "or are my orbs deceiving me, is that a Hill of old boots I see before my eyes? And what are those strange hunched creatures, with weird sticking-out beards, why, they're chasing down old charity shoes and shirts, all self-propelled, it seems. Look, they're hanging the footwear and stuff up in the trees."

"Just the charity gnomes at home," said Gray Owl, "they are a veritable treasure trove for all kinds of prizes, the masters of disguises and surprises. Hey!" he shouted and a hundred grinning mischievous faces stared up at the Princess and the Gray Owl, and cheered, waving old Cotswold wellies and Greek sandals at them , as they whooshed past.

"Will I ever be able to go one of these marvellous parties," asked Miriama wistfully, "look at the rags I'm in!"

"That's where we're going now, to fix that déshabillé of yours."

The Gray Owl flew on to a steep-sided, wooded valley. There were magic fountains which changed all the time into arching rainbow bridges in the cascading spray. Down and down they flew until a huge grotto flashed open before them, lit with a thousand candles in everlasting brilliant twilight. Gray Owl pointed out the vast silvery lake in the middle. On it floated lilies of gold leaf, all crowded with members of the Fair Folk tribe, with golden, whirring, gossamer wings. They were now standing at the head of, yes, a cat-walk, around which sat all her favourite stars, her top singers, actors, her champion childhood idols, from Burton to Jagger, alive or dead!

"My dearest and best!" she exclaimed, "I really am so lucky. Hello, everyone! I have been chosen, Gray Owl, I deserve this, I must say, for all the despicable domestic pain I've been through."

"You do, and don't forget this is your birthday, after all, and your very first. We must make up for all the lost birthday parties!" He motioned towards the cat-walk.

"No," she gasped, "I can't walk there, just look at me!"

"Trust me, trust your Dad, trust the book of life, Princess. Now step off my back, close your eyes and walk. Go on!"

Miriama closed up her eyes, pushed one foot forward, then another until she was gliding down the stage like a prize Arabian yearling. When she reached the end, she opened her eyes and found she was wearing a stunning dress of many colours as beautiful as any which the Fair folk wore. On her feet were slippers of rainbow satin which glittered in the moonlight.

"And now," cried Gray Owl, "the parade of all the birthdays you have ever missed!" At once a procession of boats and rafts appeared and glided passed the Princess, carrying every rank of celebrant, both of high and low degree, packed with more of her favourite stars, followed by Punch and Judies, Wizards, Merlin himself, Conjurors from five continents, naughty monkeys from every zoo, the ice-cream Polar Bears from every stand, the birds of the air and the animals, in two by two formation, all for the little Princess Miriama. But on the starboard side, were the processions of black-backed fiends, all in beguiling, hideous human form. What a gigantic con! She had seen it all on TV. But she didn't care. It was still so very real! What a coming out party! The dolphins leapt up out of the water, whistling with joy at the little Princess as in the Florida Everglades, another con. And the Fair Folk chorused as they turned to leave, "Happy *birthdays*, Little Princess Miriama!" They knew she wasn't a real princess, but what the heck!? Her Daddy loved her too.

"Not a melancholic in sight, See. Are we contented with our lot?"

"We are!" they chorused in unison.

"Now," said Gray Owl "one last thing - all these candles, blow them out."

"But there are thousands!"

"Have faith in the Book of Life, however close to death!"

Miriama closed her eyes, thought of her Dad, and gave one big blow.

All the guests, both invited and gate crashers, faded and vanished, leaving only the sounds of tinkling laughter in the air. She was so cast down, that was about the last thing she wanted to hear. But Daddy would fix it all when he came back.

Gray Owl saw the sky was getting lighter.

"Up on my back now," said Gray Owl.

Miriama snuffled. Was the dream all over now?

"Don't grant those two swinish domestic claimants the privilege of a single tear of yours," Gray Owl comforted her, "hellish Hemlock and devilish Manexora are out of sight for the moment, you'll see."

He took off first time and they swooped into the night along the old trajectory, but all the venues below were now closed and bound in blackness. The universe was asleep. Gray Owl circled the dark Tower twice, just to show the Princess that there were people in the book of life who were not afraid of the black side. He openly gave them the middle-finger sign, the bastards, in their banqueting hall, where sounds of disgusting revelry at night were contiguous. Then he wheeled away and landed by the window. A flock of sparrows dashed out just as they entered the gloomy chamber. Miriama gasped, again. The feathers were nowhere to be seen, they were all nestling inside the bolsters Manexora might ever need, piled up on the bed - also for the comfort, she supposed, of her cruel, highly sexed Count Hemlock. Yes, a fearless farewell gesture from herself and her allies, the sparrows, was all that was needed! Little Miriama rushed to the window, stuck her hand out, and gave her own authentic version of the two-fingered salute! Down with the utterly ungainly upstart, Manexora, and her grisly consort, Count Hemlock. "God bless you, Daddy!" she shouted into the woods and wide spaces of night. "Don't give in, dear Daddy, you'll make it, and I'll be waiting for you!"

Gray Owl raised a mighty wing, "Vive le vrai roi, Sa majeste Kariad et sa vrai Princesse, Miriama!"

The Day of the Quail

A short story (4,500 words)

by

DEDWYDD JONES

The Day of the Quail

People said it was an odd day, but for Bryn Jones it was quite normal. He was walking down the High Street of the dilapidated, emptied, ghost settlement of Pentre Ifan in the glorious far West of rural Wales, Bryn's home town, a place visitors avoided on sight. The countryside however was still inhabited, but mainly by employees of the vast National Park, fugitive academics searching for Arthur's Seat amid the crags and caves above the waves down the coast, elusive native hill farmers with their tasty sheep, and crowds of back-packing hikers and trekkers out for an elevated environmental thrill.

Bryn reached the run-down market square, the decayed heart of the dying town. The square was infested by hords of bats in the belfry of the boarded up church, which no Pest Controller seemed to notice or care much about. Next door stood an old Victorian library building with a prominent notice on the front door announcing its closure and imminent destruction. Its replacement was to be a squat Tesco store, limited by space but perfect fodder for shrinking Pentre Ifan. The old grammar school-house opposite was now used as an occasional hall for the Women's Institute and Boy Scout meetings. The few shop front windows were strewn with empty files, discarded free newspapers, uncollected mail and broken office equipment. The shops which were still open were laid out with sorry displays of second-hand goods, cheap chipped pottery, cracked glassware, garments donated from the dead and buried, smelling of washing powder and decomposition. The goods seemed to go in circles, from the needy to the needless, all on a summer's day. Business was sluggish as usual.

Bryn said a prayer as he passed the stripped, rejected library. He looked with distaste at the sole pub, the Rising Sun - more like 'setting,' Bryn muttered to himself. It dispensed stale beer, at inflated prices, when open. Its woodwork was unpainted and peeling, old mottled brown Victorian tiles glistened on the outside walls. Close by was a nescaffé caff, with creaking chairs, stained table tops, unswept floors, the local refuge of the burgeoning body of myriad pauper oldies. Around every entrance of these sad emporiums, open or closed, were chocolate wrappers and ripped newssheets whirling in the wind. The few stalls in the open area in front were laid out with plastic bric-a-brac 'bargains,' tinny kitchen utensils all the way from Tashkent, one-pound children's book-gifts also found in the cancer and heart attack shops. The stall-holders, mostly sat vacant-eyed on their wobbly, camping stools, rubbing their empty, mittened hands from time to time, reaching for the ever present comforting cup o'char close by. Other sellers sounded maniacally cheerful as they yelled out the virtues of their bedraggled cabbages and carrots and the supremacy of their mattresses and mesh curtains.

To the sense of helplessness of both shoppers and stall-holders, was added the seemingly universal physical deformity of obesity. In all his travels Bryn had never seen such waves of lapping fat, bulging bellies, massively drooping buttocks, of both men and women. Their ballooning clothes, he noted, were either straight out of the charity shops or going straight in to them. Their shopping baskets were never full of food, but packed with boxes of dinky donuts, cream slices, chicken nuggets , crisps - 'caviar to the general' !

Bryn looked around for greengrocer Ben, everybody's favourite. There he was, sitting among his pomegranites, setting out his Spanish grapes and English strawberries. Tall lean, bald and a grandfather, he was invariably cheerful, one of God's genuine genial souls. "How's it going?" asked Bryn. "Great," said Ben with enthusiasm, "they can't get enough of my pomegranites!".

"And your kids? "

"One boy's just passed his A's, the other got accepted at College, and my girl's going into nursing. All decided this morning, so it's good day to you." He doffed his peaked cap, and laughed. It was a totally genuine sound of pure joy, one hundred per cent, and reflected his celebration of the ups and downs of life, come what may. But Bryn knew Ben's old Mam had just died in hospital, of lack of nutrition it was said; one son had just been charged with drug possession, the other with GBH, and the girl transported to hospital, with her new baby, after a suspected overdose. Bryn knew too, as everyone at the market did, that Ben was on the brink of bankruptcy and had spent the last two weeks in a tent in the woods with his sons. Today he was finally emerging. He confided to Bryn that he had now found a marvellous old period cottage in the Vale for his deserving, supportive family. Bryn bought half a dozen pomegranites, laughed along with Ben at the dolorous pedestrians who looked sick and tired of just about everything, but, they both noted, some of them wore happy expressions, "like grins on huge boiled eggs" Ben remarked, but in a very sympathetic manner. Bryn moved on with a goodbye wave, feeling better, as everyone did, after a chat with the beaming Ben. If only, he thought, the large ones of the world could laugh at their own condition like the grand old greengrocer.

Bryn bought the gardening gloves he was after and stuffed them into his pocket. The flower displays were already wilting in the dried-out display buckets. The owners would be abandoning them at the end of the day. Most of the folk knew there was little future here, a grimy fading patch on the poisonous trail left by burned-out coal tips and exhausted mines, peopled by queer and fading ghosts. The sole compensation, Bryn thought, was that the entire population seemed to be quietly going nuts, quite amiably, a condition Bryn thought both fitting and worthy of mirth. He luxuriated in these states of mild moon-madness whenever he encountered them, indeed occasionally making his own original contributions.

Bryn glanced at the library, then came to an abrupt halt. An affectionate smile spread over his face. Emerging from the doors was his father, 'the Dad', the most respected man in town, retired school head teacher, local historian and scholar. He refused to move away from the place, the area where his forbears had lived and which was full of the beloved histories he always wrote up as short stories. The family lived on the outskirts of town in Hendre, 'Home,' and it was. Bryn was taking his annual holiday from teaching.

"Hi, Dad!" he called out. 'The Dad' paused and looked his son up and down as if for the first time. "Boy," he finally said, "there is only one thing wrong with you, your legs are too short for your body."

Bryn looked down at his stunted extremities. "Well, well," he said. "I think you're right again. More books?" He gestured at the plastic shopping bag the Dad was carrying.

His father nodded, "there is no end to families in all genealogies," he said, "especially ours."

"There's an end to libraries, Dad."

"But not of books." He raised the bag.

"Then let's get a nescaffé. "

"You buy, but I won't drink," said the Dad.

"OK, then. Come on."

He ushered the Dad into the darkened hole, smelling of yesterday's re-used Brazilian grains, the counter tended by a girl scarcely out of single-figure age, but she was cheerful among the slops. Dad settled down in a rickety chair. "Your Mam wants you to stay longer," he said.

"Thanks Dad, I was just thinking of that. I'll give the College a ring. It'll be OK."

"You like it in this town?"

"The Land of my Fathers."

"You've made my day, boy," he said, "I like it too."

He had called his son 'boy' all his life and had often declared for all to hear that he wasn't going to change the term, however old and gray Bryn might become.

Bryn laughed softly. He loved his little family, so full of affection and 'funny little ways' as his Mam put it.

"How's the hip," Bryn asked.

"My replacement is a treat, don't need a cane any longer, "said the Dad with a chuckle. "I was so lucky, you see. And I don't tire of telling you, or anyone, come to that – the luck of it - just going into the one-pound store to buy my cigarettes, slipped on the steps – crunch! I heard the old hip-bones crack, boy! When I tried to move, it sounded like twigs snapping off a branch. I was in dire straits. Lucky? That store was directly opposite the hospital. They carried me over to the A and E. They operated immediately. In two hours I was outside again, on my way home. Lucky, you see, they'd caught me while I was still warm," he added with a wink, "and I haven't smoked since! One of life's little triumphs, and for once of my own doing!"

Bryn loved the Dad's little stories, and followed him in that tendency.

"I had another funny experience too, Dad. I was walking down by the old estate where they're pulling up the cracked paving stones, and I saw our old neighbour old Mr Smith across the road, he waved to me. I couldn't cross over because of the traffic. I carried on walking. So did he. He suddenly stopped and pointed down at his feet, then at mine. I saw I was standing on the space where a paving stone had been removed. The space had been filled in with cement. I stared and froze. Someone had scrawled letters into the cement which was now solid. Those two letters were 'B J,' my initials, Dad. I was standing on myself. When I looked up, Mr Smith had disappeared. I thought he'd passed away, I think Mam said."

"He did," said the Dad, "there's many a fulfilled genealogy in these parts. It's funny, your story reminds me of when I was in the army. I was an interviewing officer on a WOSB, War Office Selection Board. Our job was to vet the officer cadets to see if they were the right type to go on to be commissioned. Well, one of my fellow officers was Tom Harris, and he asked the candidates just one question. "Describe your uniform, especially the lower garments, like trousers. Yes, say 'trousers.'" We remained straight-faced as the cadets limped through this final crazy test of their competence to become officers. I never saw Tom again for thirty years. Well, I met him at the final Regimental do last month, only time he ever came, and I asked him, "Why did you ask all those cadets to say 'trousers', Tom?" "You can always tell," he said, "'trousers' like that," he pronounced it with a slow, peculiar drawl, "officer material." He then walked out of the Mess, never to return."

"Really?" Bryn managed through the smiles.

"You see, Bryn," the Dad went on, "there are indeed a few answers to some of the pretty crazy questions in our fruitcake life, ones which wise men have found an answer to, but that certainly was not one of them – it was basically, a stray event of nil resolution. We shall never know the truth about Tom's 'trousers.'"

"Tell me, Dad, come on! You know."

"Think on it, boy."

"I will not leave this place in a state of suspended enlightenment, Dad," he declared.

"Oh, yes, you will" the Dad replied, "like the rest of us, and like it."

Bryn got the point. "Dad if I can ask you one last thing, why is that after looking at me long enough, people sometimes begin throwing stones?"

"Don't worry, boy," he replied "just the inexplicable pebbles of life." He smiled his ironic, comforting smile, a man of fun, kindness and talent. Bryn loved his old Dad.

"Thanks for the messcaffé," he said gesturing at the disgusting liquid stewing in the cups, "I'm off to the books now. Don't be late for dinner. Mam's got your special rice pudding."

Bryn embraced him. The Dad looked him up and down again, this time approvingly, and left. Bryn followed a few moments later.

He stood at the worn-out denim and jeans stall in front of the old shell of a school house and watched his Dad out of sight. Everyone he passed, greeted him. The Dad was a much loved man.

He decided on a quick beer before going home and went into the public bar of the awful Rising Sun. The interior was dark, the curtains unwashed, the windows uncleaned, the shelves undusted. It stank as much of urine as yesterday's beer. 'Christ,' he thought, they really should shut this place up.' Although it was market day, there were few customers - a well-dressed, middle-aged woman, with an air of refinement, sat by the window looking out. Her red hair fluffed out, her face free of cosmetics. Bryn wondered what she was doing in this spit-pit of a place. She seemed to be waiting for someone. At a corner table sprawled a dishevelled drunk, his head resting on his arms, snoring lightly, but somehow inoffensively. Another customer, a small, restless, dark creature, simian and vocal, was pacing up and down, occasionally pausing to slap the counter with the heavy metal ring on his finger - 'crack!' There was no sign of anyone behind the bar, except an Alsatian which gave a single bark every time the man hammered on the counter. The door to the back led to some ghastly interior torture chamber no doubt. The apeman now drained his pint, looked around at the comatose, indifferent clientele, and went into a wild harangue: "There are basically only two forms of music, good and evil. The Beatles are good, the Rolling Stones, evil. Left hand, right hand. One evil, one good. Mozart good, Schubert evil. One a family man, the other a syphilitic. Like that. Left, right. I explain that at the station every time, even to the police physician. I have two mistresses, one good one evil. No one has ever seen them. Who am I to say that? Well, here is my passport! "He slapped it down on the counter. "I am privy to many secrets. Look at the last page. It is in German, is it not? This is Adolf Hitler's last testament. Cunning schweinhunt to put it in my passport. No one is aware of this. I speak five languages, so I should know. Write something in my passport. Go on, something good, something evil. 'I love Good, I love Evil,' for example. Beatles, Rolling Stones, Schubert, Mozart. Here!" He abruptly concluded his babble and shouted at the bottles, "half a bitter right now!" The dog at once leapt into life, going for the noisy one, its paws scrabbling on the wooden top, its jowls slavering. The apeman bolted for the door before the beast could get to him. As he rushed out, he nearly bowled over young Geraint, the gentle giant, the family gardener, friend of horticulturists everywhere. Geraint looks down mildly at the precipitate nutcase.

"Hi, Geraint!" Bryn said, still trying to get to grips with good and evil."

"Listen," Geraint said, joining him at the bar, "this morning I went on a quail hunt. In my garden. Cunning, knows all the escape routes that quail, you can see the track lines, holes in the hedge. Never seen one close up before. This time right in the middle, no way out. Beautiful, got a crest, a purple crest. I move forward to grab it. Suddenly it shoots straight up into the air, right up, and flies to the topmost branch and settles down so no one can see him. He sleeps there. Quail lay in their nests, very tiny eggs, very expensive. Well, next moment, I was wandering about, south-west or so of my pond at the bottom of the garden, and I spot an egg in the grass! Kind of pale blue, like a small ceramic bowl. But when I looked closer, I knew, this was not a quail egg, this was a duck egg. I tell you, that bird knows what it's doing, all to put me off its track. I tell you, I've never been so disappointed. "You can eat the egg," Bryn suggested, "No," he said, "I could never do that, I wanted those birds for my little aviary. Then we could all stare at each other and wonder what it's all about. What a disappointment!" The 'drunk' woke at this point, stared through sleepy eyes at Geraint, then focused on Bryn. He immediately leapt to his feet, rushed over and began shaking Bryn's hand vigorously , "Hello there, Fergus, lad!" exclaimed the man excitedly, "Why didn't you tell us you was coming?" He had a strong Irish brogue and was quite sober. "What you doing over here?"

"I'm sorry to disappoint you," Bryn said, "I'm not Fergus!"

"But you are Fergus, Fergus Sweeney of County Cork, everyone knows that!"

"Except me," Bryn said, "ask Geraint here. Do I look like someone else, Geraint?"

"Not that I know of," said Geraint with quiet conviction. "He's Bryn Jones of Sir Penfro. I do his Dad's garden. Honest!"

The man gaped again at Bryn, "a spitting image! You got a doppelganger on the loose, mate. I'd better pass on the word, OK."

With a last, long astonished look, he backed out of the front door. As if on cue, the seated lady now came to life, blinked, and began, in turn, to stare at Bryn, wrinkling her brows. She appeared to be trying to remember some distant, forgotten matter. Finally, she moved purposefully across to him, still staring hard, until her face was only an inch away from his. Bryn remained stationary. Where after all, could he go? She suddenly shook her flaming curls and her puzzled expression faded for a moment.

"What in the hall has this day got in store for me now?" Bryn wondered.

"You've come for the market, haven't you?" the woman asked, her voice surprisingly gentle. Bryn nodded. It was true.

"We have many markets here. I don't think you'll be disappointed."

Bryn wondered if she had actually seen any of them.

Her reflective mood softened even more. She reached out and ran her fingers through his hair. "Your hair," she said, "so soft and silky, and falls, see here, in folds like, like the buds of a hyacinth."

"The buds of a hyacinth," repeated Geraint who had been listening intently, "I like it."

A sudden look of realization mixed with rapture spread over her face.

"My God, is it you? You are really one, aren't you?" She seized Bryn's hand," I know who you are!" She pressed his hand against her breast. "Yes, I can feel it, the electricity, like a brand in my heart, the magnetism of the songs of ancient sun-rays rising in me, and I'm not making it up. You are one of the ancient ones, from way back, the eld, come back to greet us over the ages. Can you feel that glow?" she pressed his hand to her breast again, "My God it's running right through me!" She shivered with delight. "Where do you come from? Where?!" she asked, still rapt.

"Carmarthen," he confessed,

"Carmarthen!" I knew it!" she sang out, "Merlin's town! You have come back to tell us. Feel it! I feel it. You have come back to tell us all."

"Yes, yes…" Bryn responded, his words lacking any meaning, but feeling her passion and vision, "Yes, yes, you do," she said, embracing him, holding his hand to her breast again. She finally drew apart, shuddering with pleasure, her face glowing, her eyes shining. He felt her warmth radiate his whole body. She gave him a sighing hug of farewell, kissed him on both cheeks, turned, and in a trice was gone.

Geraint blinked, "Dammo," he exclaimed, "that was a pleasant experience, that was!" and hurriedly followed her out.

Bryn leaned against the bar and thought of the ancient bards, Merlin the Enchanter, and his enigmatic Red-Haired wraiths. Going great, he thought. But when was he going to be served. The dog had now disappeared. And, yes, Geraint was right, it had been a pleasant experience. Bryn slowly moved outside. He found himself gazing at the blooms of the flower stall. The stall-holder was sitting by his dog, a massive mastiff, where do they all come from, he wondered. The hairy hulk was tethered to a lamppost, its huge head lolling from side to side as if about to fall off. For some reason, Bryn felt for his gardening gloves in his pocket. He nodded to the stall holder, who turned away and sipped his char. Quick as a whippet, without any warning, the dog darted forward. Before he could move out of the way, the hound snuffled its snout directly into Bryn's pocket, seized one of the gloves, and retreated behind the lamppost, the gardening gauntlet between its teeth. Bryn moved to retrieve it. The dog shook its hairy locks, snapped at him in warning, then settled down, the glove between its paws. It then proceeded to tear it to pieces, finger by finger, it seemed, glancing at him, as if daring him to act. Bryn stood his ground and gazed, bemused. Even the dogs were now apparently suffering from the universal dementia of the town. When all that remained was a tangled pile of chewed up fabric, the slavering beast stopped masticating and stared up at Bryn. Bryn remained resolutely still. He swore a look of disappointment came into the eyes of the hound. Bryn smiled. He had won. He had not given the dog the satisfaction of losing control and fighting back. He had lost the glove but he had won the war. The stall-holder had looked on through the whole episode with a dead-eye, fish-like expression. He had made no effort to curb the piratical mutt from its plunder or to apologise. Bryn decided he would terminate this savage canine provocation with a suitable, more subtle riposte.

"Here," he said to the stall-holder, "he seems to fancy gloves, so give him this one as well," and handed him the second glove. The stall-holder fondly ruffled the dog's great ugly head, and began feeding the mad beast its second five-fingered feast of the day, fondly watching it chomping and tearing away. Bryn nodded, and moved off. Yes, everything happily concluded, to the satisfaction of all the participants, smiles on their faces, including the dog's.

Bryn suddenly realised he had forgotten his bag of pomegranites somewhere. Should he go back for them? No, he decided - anyway, one of the unbalanced dogs of the town would have probably eaten them by now. He decided to wend his way home through the outskirts of the shrinking town, the abandoned no-man's land where few inhabitants cared to venture. He felt like some watcher of the Lees, a casual overseer of deserted scrublands. The place was dotted with varieties of industrial rot - ruined workshops, collapsed huts, a single smashed railway carriage, the rusting iron skeletons of fallen sheds. Piles of brick-bats and fallen slates and masonry made up the rubble that lay everywhere. He surveyed the seized up pulleys , the smashed security lights, the flattened gates and broken chains, all still in place, vandalized but unstolen. And to tease the mind further, a tumbledown pigeon-loft sunk in a stinking oily pool. Clinker pathways led everywhere and nowhere. Bryn picked his way through the black sacks of kitchen waste, the fat-trap dumps, the stained mattresses and sofas. The surface was spread everywhere with purple mires, troughs, lagoons of oxidising chemicals, leaching from the piles of spoil. He paused as he left the last blasted gateway of the old 'new town' and its blight-lands, and stepped onto the path, leading home. Both sides were lined with blooming clouds of Hawthorn, his and Geraint's favourite floral route to Hendre. The blood-shot alders and elderberry trees, seemed immune to chemical contagion. They were spreading happily over the whole of the toxic meadows. He sniffed the abundant buddleias crowded with cabbage whites, giving off a pervading, fragrant perfume. The ground was covered with yellow ragwort, mayweeds, creeping buttercups, and the ubiquitous cranesbills. They all merged together, all the scents, the colours and the shifting serene images, all brightness and fertility among the buds and blossoms. He stopped to listen to the grasshoppers, the chiff-chaffs, the warblers and song thrushes, especially the greater honey-guide golden oreoles, rare in these parts, friend of the buzzing bee everywhere. He felt the dreadful graveyard with its disintegrating industrial tombstones had again been overshadowed by the simple spots of sunny greenery around him. He felt a rush of pleasure. Yes, even the two-ton, gloomy, pear-shaped inhabitants, must share in it, "nature is generous as well as ubiquitous with its treasures" - the Dad's words; the Red Head happy in her dreams of Merlin; Ben laughing in his tent, canonized once more; Mr Smith back from the dead; Fergus finally laid to rest; Geraint over the moon with the hyacinth; Adolf's last testament finally exposed; all the pets in the world ever so nice; all the stall-holders sharing their cuppa, sullenness banished; even the foul Nescafe joint and the hideous 'Rising', had performed an useful social function; and no more stonings on top of it! Amazing satisfactions all round! As he approached Hendre, the hawthorn bushes seemed to swell up like clouds and burst with all the sweets of paradise. What a day!

He strode along, assured that "the subtle magic which is inevitable in the most mystifying scheme of things, has its place even in benighted Pentre Ifan," as the Dad had observed recently. Bryn increased his pace as he thought of home, his Welsh 'Hendre.' His Mam was waiting at the front gate. She hugged him and gave him a big kiss, her eyes shining, "so you're staying a few days longer, Bryn. Lovely." She took his arm and led him indoors.

"Did you have a good day?"

"Just… about normal, Mam."

"Have you decided on a name for it yet?"

"Got a bit of a choice, 'The Day of the Ancient Bard,' 'The Day of the Torn Gauntlet' or 'The Day of the Quail,' which one, Mam?"

"We've used 'bard' before, I don't know about 'gauntlet', so, - 'The Day of the Quail.'"

"So be it then!"

"Now, love, come and have some of my nice rice pudding before your Dad eats it all up."

THE GRAVE DIGGERS

or

'Nil by Mouth'

a satire for the stage (60 mts)

by

DEDWYDD JONES

Dedwydd Jones

In memory of all the avoidable deaths in English hospitals 2008-2013, before and beyond

With gratitude to

'Toten Gräber Lied'

by

Schubert

<u>CAST</u>:
BILLY ZEE ZEE, 1st Grave Digger, the Boss

STAN S.S, 2nd Grave Digger, BILLY's Aide

PISSY LIZZY, Nurse, BILLY'S girl friend

FRED EVANS, Reporter

(*Midnight; graveyard, outlines of gravestones; dead flowers in jars; a few graves open, with piles of soil; outline of yew trees, left; owls hoot; up 10 seconds of The Death March, fades; up left, building, with sign 'West Wing Psychiatric Unit'; another sign on adjoining building, 'Accident and Emergency, entrance'; centre back, sign reads 'Chapel', above, illuminated crucifix; next on left, sign on wall reads 'Crematorium', with chimney stack, smoke rising; right front, sign reads 'Car Park'; left front running to back, hedge; all signs lit up in flickering lights; front stage, pile of body bags; wooden coffin used as table, with forms, clip-board, rubber stamps, documents, pair of binoculars, bottles of booze, various costumes and masks, paints and brushes, used as indicated; wheel-barrow with 'body' (a dummy) in body-bag, leg dangling over side; bedside table, with vase of water with rotten flowers, a buzzer; by graves, old fashioned candle-lanterns; two gravediggers, BILLY ZEE ZEE, and his mate, STAN S.S. in holes, in overalls, lean on shovels, panting; sound of ambulance, police sirens, screeching of tyres, vehicle doors slamming, alarmed shouting; dogs barking; owls hooting; BILLY points at crematorium; both clamber out of holes, tip the 'corpse' into grave; put another 'corpse' in wheel-barrow; BILLY points at coffin; they dip into costumes, BILLY puts on white coat and stethoscope of doctor, with benign mask; STAN puts on saintly mask, straw hat, Vicar dog's collar, holds a pocket bible, makes sign of cross over audience; masks are on the end of elastic so they can be raised and lowered around neck; BILLY, STAN occasionally swig from bottle, do farewell dance to corpses, change back into overalls, continue digging; ambulance siren, screech of brakes off stage; BILLY looks at signs and sounds through binoculars*)

BILLY ZEE ZEE: Christ, another hearse - charged with the aged, no doubt! *(BILLY looks at clip-board, adds a note)*

STAN: What's the score now, Billy Zee Zee?

BILLY: Thousands of people here have been identified as corpses. *(Consults clip-board, looks round with binoculars)* We'll be full again at dawn.

STAN: True sadness is a shovel in a grave without a corpse.

BILLY: In melancholy vein today, Stan. *(Addresses dummy 'corpse' in body bag in wheelbarrow, laughing)* so pull yourself together, mate, and give us a laugh!

STAN: *(to corpse)* Come on there, shake a leg!

BILLY: Shake, baby, shake!

STAN: He's so full of himself.

BILLY: Now don't be lazy just because you're dead. *(Kicks wheel-barrow. Leg falls off. Both roar with laughter)*

BILLY: Him and his bloody burst vessels.

STAN: Christ, he's gone all rigid.

BILLY: That's because he's run out of fresh blood!

STAN: A real hoot. In my last ward, Slaughterhouse 8, everyone developed 'C Difficile,' my favourite leveller, all perished, like him here.

(Owl hoots; they roar with laughter, dance with the leg, hoot like owls)

STAN: *(to corpse)* I'm doublin' up with mirth, mate! We need a laugh. But where is our Pissy Lizzie? She enjoys our dance of the sugar-plum stiffs!

BILLY: *(Looking through binoculars)* And where are our guardians, guards, security agents, porters, bouncers..? Have to send you out again on patrol, Stan, we've got to get it right.

STAN: Leave it to me.

BILLY: So many, runners, jumpers, escapees, flat-liners, keep them on their toes, Stan. They said, ' it's got to be outcomes-based before we can take mortality measures.'

STAN: God knows, there' a demise crisis on, and all they do is complain about milk deliveries.

BILLY: Our dairy products are the finest in Europe, ask the Gerries – 'bug frei!'

(NOISES OFF)

STAN: …look over there, Billy, behind the bloody hedge, and up by the ovens, and next to the morgue, placards by the score.

BILLY: Not the grief mob again.

STAN: See, up and down, up and down!

BILLY: *(Looking through binoculars, reads out)* Placards is right... hundreds...

STAN: ...what do they say today?

BILLY :   *(Reading out through binoculars)* 'Dignity for the Elderly.'

STAN: 'Prats for twats!

BILLY: So what? It was ever thus.

STAN: And over there - by the old Victorian charnel house...

BILLY: *(Reads)* ... 'Patient safety is top of the tree!' - deadly nightshade no doubt. *(THEY laugh)*

STAN: And by the new crematorium now ... *(Reading out)* ...'Down with gangrene!'

BILLY: How obscene!

STAN: *(Reading)* 'Re-appear the dis-appeared...'

BILLY: What a vapid plea!

STAN: *(Reading)* 'Out with wrongly labelled demises!'

BILLY: Such banalities! And, the terminal hoot, folks,

(reading, to audience) 'Transparency is real!' *(roars with laughter. Reads)* Listen! 'Save our Ma's!' 'Cure our Pa's!' They're out - the Blight of the Bereaved is upon us again, curse their rotten socks. I tell you now, Stan, buddy, SS, I know what malignancy is at the bottom of all this – Grief! Worse than any cancer!

STAN: The shifty swine. Go on, Billy.

BILLY: *(Reading placard)* 'When things are going wrong, you need to shine a very bright light on it.' Christ, that is going to raise the dead, isn't it!

STAN: I'll take my spade to them!

BILLY: Yes, that'll elevate the turnover, too. Stan, it's not the slaughter, it's the sentimentality.

STAN: But they are real people, aren't they?

BILLY: Flesh, fur and faeces, mate, not a dummy in the lot. Unreal but, true, mate. We are fundamentally just a wonderful production line of living human meat.

STAN: Bless you, my son! Now bring on Pissy Lizzy, our top specialist in hand relief!

BILLY: Pissy Lizzy, what a gal! Her 'Do not Resuscitate Notices' are so motherly, they are totally convincing!' And what a mortician! See her masks? Epiglottis as good as new, rosy cheeks, the hint of a smile, the Giaconda of the tombs.

And the Loved Ones, they adore Lizzy's work, 'so life-like' they gasp between sobs, 'looks ten years younger.' That's a marvellous gift, make the dead ones grin, and live ones pay for the skin!' She's good as our egregious Dr Shipman was, and he knew what he was doing!

STAN: Her last 'nil to mouth' was a winner . *(Tells the story)* In her cubicle, dehydrated octogenarian, grey to the lips, gums distended, so Pissy stuffs a catheter up his arse, fills him full of porridge till he bursts and reports death due to a dislocated shoulder blade. *(Roars of laughter)*

BILLY: But she started with an advantage - she could hardly speak English, although she was English. But after a few lessons on her knees before me she soon learned to talk posh. Yes, yes, yeeeeess! That was me!

STAN: Hey, look, Billy, the placards – they're on the move.

BILLY: *(Looking through binoculars, points)* There's one!

STAN: What?

BILLY: And another! They always go in two's, like fuckin' thievin' magpies.

STAN: Who?

BILLY: Whistle-blowers, of course!

STAN: How can you be sure they're whistle-blowers?

BILLY: Smell 'em on the wind, mate, 'specially when the smoke is risin'.

Let me tell you,

Regulators and Watchdogs,

Are piss-poor fools,

They invent and ignore

Impossible rules!

STAN: Yes, yes, Doctor. But Mother Church adores Pissy Lizzie's other great art too - gagging. When she closes her mouth, nothing gets out, and that goes for her patients as well, of course. If they don't have a cleft chin when they arrive, they certainly have one when they leave. We're all gagged, to a greater or lesser extent.

BILLY: A defective syllogism! - except us.

STAN: That's what I meant.

BILLY: And after the gag moral, you have the universal gob-stopper, cash.

STAN: *(Dancing with leg)* Here, it's the whirly-gig of time…it never stops!

BILLY: Like us again! Our dominions, watch towers,

protectorates, compounds, dispensations, laagers, Concentration Camps…er… **concentrated** Camps – our spelling – bone-orchards and work houses, are spreading all over the land. *(They punch the air, cheer)* I even noted with my blind eye certain messages of ugly conciliation, 'The risk to Managers is made greater by not meeting the highest expectations.' And I conceded, 'I grant that the public has every right to know where the canteen soup plates are stored.' What could be more 'entente cordiale-ish?' But look at them now, brainless liturgies all the way! *(Vehicle revvs from Car Park. BILLY looks through binoculars)* Another body drop! Unforgivable! We're so overstretched! *(Points at corpse)* Ask him!

STAN: *(Shouts at vehicle)* No more talks! Get outta in here, Billy, I'll brain the bloody thing.

BILLY: No, cool it, Stan, put down the cricket bat, and look! That's not an ambulance, that's the Boss's Rolls Royce.

STAN: Can it be? So many… the Chief Porter's, the Top Exec's, the Sanitary Commander's, shit, you can't see no difference, I mean £211,000 per anus, minimum, with gold-plated pensions. Whose Rolls is whose Rolls, I ask you?

BILLY: Stan, stick to the stakes, and you'll get yours too.

STAN: I better, or it's their guts for garters, and I means that literal, mate.

BILLY: Pass the scalpel.

(Squeals from centre back. ENTER PISSY LIZZY, in nurses' uniform, early-twenties, petite, gorgeous, sexy voice, in tight nurse's uniform, garter-belt flashes, carries pillow case of dirty, bloodied hospital garments, bandages, dragging 'PATIENT' (dummy) along by the hair, kicking it, spitting at it, 'PATIENT' in shitty pyjamas, around ankles, dripping with 'piss,' PISSY LIZZY kicks 'PATIENT' in crotch)

LIZZY: *(loud and sexy)* I will no longer put up with your filthy piss and shit on my hands ever again!

(Wipes her hands on the PATIENT'S Hair. STAN, BILLY look on approvingly)

LIZZY: *(To 'PATIENT')* I told you again and again, 'Nil by Mouth!'' You are no longer a human being, you are an animal, an animal! Look, Billy, dirty diarrhoea all under my finger nails. I know there's a shortage of body bags, but please, my Willy Billy, please get one on it right away.

BILLY: Why? He's dead already.

LIZZY: And to think I let him drink all the rose water from the vase when he was as dry as a bone. He suffered initially from reaction to chicken nuggets, but his hydration level was fine, the hypocrite. Cause of death – spurious pneumonia. From now on the universal watchword is 'No medication, No resuscitation!' And I do not mind flinging about the belongings of a corpse if he really deserves it, like this one. Billy Zee Zee, Stan SS, to your to your neat final solutions now, pack him up for good!

BILLY: Well, since it's little old bouncy dancy you...
(STAN and BILLY try to force 'PATIENT' into body bag. They give up)

BILLY: What an ill shape.

STAN: Fuckin recalcitrant!

(Leave 'body' half in bag, half out. BILLY consults clip-board)

BILLY: Plot 41745 over there. Drop her in it, my Pissy Lizzy.

PISSY LIZZY: Thanks, my dizzy hero!

(LIZZY drags PATIENT to grave. Looks down hole)

LIZZY: Hey, there's another one in here already.

BILLY: It's the cuts, we're having to double up. And I predict by next week we'll be doing triples.

STAN: Bloody foul pong again, so many undone – thank God!

LIZZY: You're right, piled them up after their ops I did, in the chapel, label on every big toe, human rights respected, up to the altar, then higher, up to the crucifix, bloody thing.

STAN: Come to Jesus! Ha, ha!

LIZZY: Some had even switched off their own life supports.

BILLY :   Unforgivable!

LIZZY: Makes them look so bad. The shit they leave behind! And sometimes, as you know, they were spilling out into the car park and had to be wrestled to the ground by our brave porters in full public view.

BILLY: Doing a grand job!

LIZZY: I was firm but strict with the survivors. I explained to them that their incandescent rage was due to grief and to come back to discuss it later like civilized people when they had cooled off.

BILLY: Superb psychology!

STAN: Such deep, deep empathy!

LIZZY: What I also advised the surgeons was that after all wheel-chair operations, the patients should be turned out into the streets, without directions.

STAN: That would go a long way to solving the over-crowding.

BILLY: Ignorant when lost, ignorant when found.

STAN: Spot on, Doc!

BILLY: Come on Pissy Lizzy, what's the true secret of your magical juices?

LIZZY: I just try to maintain a balanced cheerful outlook is all.

BILLY: You put Florrie Nightingale to shame, pet, my sexy dame.

LIZZY: In you go! *(Kicks PATIENT into grave, yells)* You may still have your meat jacket on but not for long, I promise you! Look, pyjamas round his ankles, showing his dirty danglers, how useless. Ugh! Not for me, only fit for the worms underfoot, see! And look *(Empties pillow-case of bloodied garments and bandages into grave)* See! And these are not his, look there, the tiny-tot nappies, held together with paper-clips, these are the cerements of a toddler. *(Of corpse)* This one is a child molester, a hospital linen filcher, a wretch to boot, on the brink of decomposition, thank Christ.

BILLY: Who was responsible for his nursing?

LIZZY: The relatives.

STAN: Outrageous. They're not even qualified.

LIZZY: His body was all grazed when they brought him in.

STAN: That was due to the dragging.

BILLY: They never look beneath the broken skin.

LIZZY: He was also admitted for vomiting but he was perambulatory. I passed him over. By the way, how do you take temperatures?

BILLY: You need never know, my love.

LIZZY: From now on, it's 'unfit for treatment' if he's got a single scratch or speck of vomit on him. *(Spits into grave)* Bloody animal! Lower class git! That's why! Shames upper class manhood beyond the grave. Dirty fuckin' erko-berko prolaterian plebothicko! He is! I know it's a terrible thing to say, but... PLEB!

STAN: Of course he is.

BILLY: You can always tell a lower-class corpse by its accent. *(LIZZY spits on corpse)* Well spattered, Pissy Lizzy. You have performed your dump so ably – hygiene done to a turn! Wicked!

LIZZY: I have put my foot down - I will never again spread toilet tissue over a pile of shit, even if it's under the bed!

STAN: We salute you! Woman, you smell of roses.

LIZZY: *(Aside)* Must be in Holy Orders, ripe twat!

BILLY: Just a quick-change nicker test now. Do it Lizzy, the pus and blood-stained coat, in the box. ('coffin.' *LIZZY puts it on, flashes her thighs.*

Introduces herself) – Mortician!

ALL: Ugh! Ugh!

BILLY: Now the white coat. *(Puts on clean white coat, flashes her thighs)* Beautician! The mask. *(LiZZY puts on pretty-nurse mask)* Miss Reassurance herself! *(ALL applaud)*

BILLY: You are an adept, my Pissy, my fabulous flasher, bless your trusty training! Now the final hurdle, your R.D.T. - Registered Diploma Tests, facile and fixed, I assure you, just going through the motions, Lizzy gal, but they will transport you to the very heart of golden increments for the remainder of your days, your own El Dorado of the Wards , without a suspicion against you, or our ilk. OK?

LIZZY: I'm behind you, sweety, with everything I've got.

STAN: And these bodies should be far more selected, younger stiffs for sexy Pissies ...

LIZZY: ... and more hymens for my Stan and Billy Boy, both ways!

BILLY: ...a Saville Row touch there!

(ALL cheer. PISSY dances with PATIENT'S leg. Drags out head and death mask from body bag. Picks up paints and brushes. Adds finishing touches to death mask. STAN, BILLY admire her work)

STAN: She is adding delightful finishing touches to her death mask.

LIZZY: And how they smile the while as I ease their dolorous clamour.

(ALL cheer. Roars, yells of rage off stage)

BILLY: The grief rioters out in force I'm afraid, Lizzy, stiffened with vile whistle-blowers.

LIZZY: *(Replaces death mask in body bag)* My masks are at the ready.

BILLY: You make them all so resurrectable looking, O Pissy one.

LIZZY: Another half dozen free wanks at dusk for you, Billy.

STAN: *(Looking through binoculars)* Christ, more cries of rage from the Anguish Anarchists.

LIZZY: Evil is all! Wait till I've finished with them!

STAN: But do not fret, Pissy, 'we, the managers, all have a clear view of who can offer genuine, stern, even merciless leadership, which is fundamental to the entire Governing Boards' ethos at this painful juncture in time!' And Billy, they meant you!

BILLY: No sweat. I always had a super plan 'B', so don't worry, Pissy Lizzy. To your qualifcatory tests first. You may be all Roedean on the outside, but inside you are one mass of bubbling, pussurating, fucking ignorance. And I will see that the whole fuckin' world soon knows it!

STAN: I second that most heartily.

LIZZIE: *(Pointing at the Cross)* May He discharge huge and most timely dividends upon your head, Billy.

BILLY: No problem.

LIZZY: I had at least one hour to learn the whole job...

STAN: ...and it worked like hell!

BILLY: Listen to the reports on your reports. Your 'nocturnal forays here, down to the last letter, one swoop, number of patients forever inert? - five-hundred zero one. All superbly rendered,' and your prime diagnosis - dementia, I see, was popular, but senility came a close second - all told with your usual irrepressible touches of humour.

LIZZIE: Half a dozen free blow jobs for you, Billy boy, before Confession or after, as you wish.

BILLY: Ta, love. Always take away my breath you do.

STAN: What about me?

LIZZIE: Oh, do close the suck hole, Stan, or take a running jump into it! Billy, I'm ready. Test my wide-ranging hospital skills, and beyond.

BILLY: *(Taps clip-board)* This patient fell off the toilet and died. C.O.D. - Cause of Death?

LIZZIE: Shingles.

BILLY: This one reached for the buzzer, carefully placed well out of reach, so fell out of bed and died. C.O.D?

LIZZIE.   Polyps in the lower colon.

BILLY: This one fell down the broom-cupboard steps. C.O.D?

LIZZIE: Sciatica.

BILLY: This one couldn't breathe any more. C.O.D?

LIZZY: Crushed gall bladder stones.

BILLY: And your recommendation for a perforated ulcer?

LIZZY: Amputation of the left leg below the knee...

BILLY: ...and got rid of two nasty varicose veins at the same time. I'll put in a special commendation for that. Little short of superb. And here, you failed to spot two carbuncles, five abscesses and a dozen bed sores, all on one child, O keen practitioner! Don't say a word, it was not for you to defend. Not your remit. You knew it, I knew it. The boorish relatives out there did not know it, the imbeciles. And they will never know it, so ignore them. *(Reads report)* So another pauper child died, so what again! *(Tears up report)* You were never supposed to explore any signs of foetal distress. And did you report your patient was bleeding to death? No!

STAN: I should bloody well think so!

LIZZY: Quite.

BILLY: Why did you refuse to mop out the toilets.

LIZZY: Fear of infection.

BILLY: Exactly!

LIZZY: Let me tell you, I am state registered, highly so, I can do light ironing, take care of child vouchers, carry out Compassion Checks in the Relief Department so none are lost due to incredible pain; collect minor refuse in a timely manner as it states in the accident book; I can do pulse jobs, scrub technician duties, catering meals, palliaitive carelessness a speciality, hospitality tasks, mirror wiping, dusting - but only chandeliers; practitioner of disabilities, late intervention officer, and all these jobs carry their own responsibility, no silly watch dogs, health and safety snoops. Not for us!

BILLY: There are more rules for bouncers and taxi-drivers than us!

LIZZY: I love that.

BILLY: So, more than anything, after one hour of intensive tests and training you were turned loose on the wards, 'just make it up as your go along' was the last word of command…

STAN: … a stroke of pragmatic genius! *(To audience)* All applaud our Pissy Lizzy.

BILLY: And I can assure you that the Strategic Health Corporations, the Care Quality Commissions, the Parent Associations, Accounts Monitors, the Childbirth and Baby Care Council, the Major Boards of Doctors, the League of Hospital Inspectors, dead or alive, even now constitute no threat, for their snouts are forever deep in the trough of the eternal gravy train, up to their ears, pelf has long ago overtaken conscience! But look, still over 300,000 hospital carers! - think of all the tenderness.

LIZZY: And I will never be paid lower that a floor sweeper! And I will never again brush the clogged dentures of the departed or clean out pressure ulcers with a single scoop! As Health and Admin Clinician, Phlebotomist, even with Porter bonus and highly paid vacation, I can push it up to four three-week holidays a year, plus overtime without the awful geriatrics, I can now buy a five-bedroomed suburban villa, so there, all you stupid, wreckers , whistle-blowers and your agony columns out there, we will prevail!

STAN: That's it! Our Lizzy's in the vanguard!

BILLY: Lizzy, one more non-trick question - all these dire and unfortunate deaths, they were all basically due to one suspiciously normal cause. Now give me one blanket C.O.D. to replace that inaccurate nomenclature. Utter it!

LIZZY: Septicaemia.

BILLY: Excellent. And why?

LIZZY: Because septicaemia is natural, comes with the body.

BILLY: And thus re-classifies all Causes of Death which were/are somehow not normal! With glorious sepsis and her sinister sister septicaemia, behold, down goes the death rate, and up go our reputation, promotions and bonuses. Keep it up, Lizzy. You've passed just about bloody well every bloody bordello examination going. No more shit or syph in your panties, Pissy Lizzy!

(A yell from the grave. ALL freeze. PISSY screams. A figure, journalist FRED EVANS, Welsh Reporter, broad accent, , struggles out of grave, peeling off body bag, covered with shit and blood; he is very drunk, staggers, falls panting)

FRED EVANS: Not yet, not yet the Man with the Scythe! Not… yet…

STAN: …Christ, is he panting!

BILLY: Too vocal for a corpse I'd say.

LIZZY: Not my fault. He was in there already. I told you

STAN: Shit, I know this two-faced sodden sot, he's the loco reporter, Fred Evans, dead drunk as only a Taff can be.

LIZZY: Be that as it may, Fred is definitely not dead.

STAN: Then he's pissed as a fart - got to be, to lie down in darkness voluntarily.

FRED: I didn't do it on purpose, like, boyos.

BILLY: Don't worry, Fred Evans, I have immense reserves of the old crinkly greens.

FRED: *(Sobering up)* Did I hear the words 'crinkly greens'?

STAN: Stand to attention when you address an officer, Evans 704.

FRED: *(Salutes BILLY, sways)* Sorry, sir. But I love paper greenery. Give me my orders, sir, any orders.

BILLY: Your orders are to accompany Billy SS here to ascertain the strength of the official forces around the perimiter. Duck, dodge and weave and co-report back here, without any hangers on, dead or alive. Then you'll hear that holy symphony - crinkly, crinkly, crinkly-green, you will have what I have seen!

FRED: There's lovely, sir.

BILLY: Off you go!

STAN: Onwards!

BILLY: To your lying duties as strategic health watchers!

LIZZY: Piss off, stinky Fred Evans, you walking beer-hall, go!

(STAN helps FRED to EXIT right back, disappear into shadows; sounds of fighting, struggling, blows; yells, ambulance sirens, screeching tyres; CUT LIGHTS; SPOT ON LIZZY and BILLY embracing; they fall into grave, strip off; sound of sex being had; winding sheets, death masks, under garments, flung out of grave as LIZZY rises to climax. RE-ENTER STAN and FRED, 'body' (dummy) clinging to STAN's back; FRED does little to help STAN; STAN struggles with the 'corpse ,' staggers over to graves; STAN finally tears limbs off back, stamps on them; turns on FRED)

STAN: Bloody turncoat bastard, why you not help me? You saw what they did. Poured jars of glue on my back and stuck on a stiff. I couldn't reach him. You could at least have done that. Why?

FRED: I was drunk, boyo, staggerin' like.

STAN: They didn't touch you with a barge-pole, did they?. How'd you feel if you had a 64 pound monkey on your back?

FRED: Asinine.

(STAN kicks 'limbs' from 'corpse' into grave; a scream; LIZZY stands up, dressing hastily)

FRED: Hey, Pissy Lizzy, can I have a fuck too?

LIZZY: We have not been introduced.

STAN: Listen. I report. We drove off the Agonizers, trounced the weepers, decimated the whiners, located the ministry terminators, and finally, stuck 'em down in the mud just here. Fucks all round I say! Especially me, 'cos Fred was drunk as a skunk, on orders I do believe, and did not help to scrape off the glue or the person I was stuck with, so I was almost stymied. Fuckin' defective condom, you are!

(BILLY rises *out of grave, dressing)*

BILLY: So they're on the run?

STAN: Yes, but in our direction.

LIZZY: I don't wish to be cohabited in this grave by any fiends, devils, or imps in any shape or form.

BILLY: Worry not. When have I ever failed to get a climax out of you in the accepted manner with a normal person? When?

LIZZY: I have never been psychologically disoriented by your lavish attentions, Billy Zee Zee!

FRED: There's lovely and affectionate, 'specially with 64 pound monkeys around.

STAN: Don't tell me, you Quisling.

FRED: Quizzle…what? So my report now. Here, listen, got my English O levels, I did in night school when day school got too rambunctious and I had to be let down by rope from the crenelated walls. But that skill remains. Good at writing I still am. What you want me to write?

BILLY: Write … nothing.

FRED: Nothing?

BILLY: That's it. Forget everything you've seen or heard of here. A blank, nothing ever happened.

FRED: There's lovely then. Just the usual, 'patient care comes first' and all that donkey stuff…but Billy Boss, I need a few extras for the whistle-blowers in disguise, they sure fool you, but never me. They've really stuck their necks out this time and the Ministry's got spies on the roof-tops out on the sly and they're moving over the ovens. I got a feeling they will rise up from the dead and worry a lot of very decent people, like your Honour and ilk, right on this damp spot.

BILLY: Say no more… *(BILLY hands FRED money)*

FRED: …thanks for the tip, I knew it was coming of course, that's why I came, how I do not know. Enough is enough, until the next time. And I did hear rumours of probes by new Inspectors rising out of the unwashed public. So, bless you, I'm off. And don't worry about the placards, soft as shit like the corpses, all melting away in the tears, ha, ha!

LIZZY: Now, fuck off out of here, you lying perv, you swindling, crooked, vicious, jumped-up little arse-licker before we chuck you back into the stinky primordial maggot-infested manure dump over there which is your real home!

FRED: Say no more! *(Aside)* What a spitting virago! - a sexy honey pot, a dodgy babe, there's lovely!

LIZZY: You're animal all over, again and again!

STAN: And don't forget to salute the Captain when you dismiss, Evans 704.

FRED: Yes sir. *(Salutes)* Report to you, report to them. Ta, ta. Whoops again! And I'll never ask Pissy for a fuck again.

BILLY: That's what I like to hear – true self-denial!

FRED: Ta ta, boyos!

(EXIT FRED EVANS running, staggering, counting money)

STAN: He's got rigor and mortis written all over him, but look at him go!

BILLY: Leave him to the dregs.

STAN: You're right, he'll never get over the outside drains.

LIZZY: He drinks at the Poisoned Spring down by the crematorium where all the Super Bug Nurses go! I'll give him 'tipple' tonight! *(ALL roar with laughter)* 'Double agent'? Double arsehole*!* You knew of course what would happen when you ordered him out.

BILLY: He'd betray us just in time, let us know when the weeping rabble were on the march, and the direction of that march.

STAN: You're cunning as a little old eel, Billy boy!

BILLY: And if he sends any of his sickly relatives into our bloody wards, they'll soon be singing with the heavenly choirs and wringing their hands like all their other loved ones! But one already on your poor back, Stan, there's his pathetic remains. And it's true, Fred is a double agent of the thick Moronites, the disgusting Expectorators, the Self-Righteous Brothers, I saw gold glitter in their palms - even now gathering for the big push, and at the end of it is…us.

LIZZY: No, no, never us. Billy, do something!

BILLY: Don't droop at the mouth, my dripping Pissy Lizzy, I told you already about my famous 'plan B.'

LIZZY: But we're all hemmed in.

BILLY: We are all hemmed out as well.

LIZZY: How'd you mean?

STAN: *(Sound of revving)* Over down by there, a vehicle.

LIZZY: Is this a Rolls I see before my eyes?

STAN: Is the Boss taking us for a ride?

BILLY: No, Stanny boy, that's not the Boss's Rolls.

STAN: The Fertility Director's? No? The Caeserean Section Experts? No? The Toilet Flush Engineers? No?

LIZZY: Come on, let's see your plonker then!

BILLY: That Rolls you see in the Car Park happens to belong to... yours truly's, me, all mine!

LIZZY: My hero!

STAN: It will surely carry us over the rainbow.

LIZZY: I love a far horizon!

BILLY: "Like a patient etherised upon a table."

LIZZY: How romantic. *(ALL dance)*

BILLY: All this is infinitely more exciting than a Coronation Street episode for terminal cases.

BILLY: Now the powers of lawlessness and disorder are on the march, large movements of slush funds are inevitable, indeed desirable. So, first order is - change dress! *(BILLY dresses in Doctor's costume, Stan in Vicar garb, put on masks; (all masks on elastic so they can be raised and lowered) LIZZY in white coat of beautician, all don suitable masks)*And grab your escape bags! *(ALL grab a small bag, they shake bags, rattle of coins)* twenty thou, small change, mere bagatelle! Now to the geography, mostly Midlands and Northlands, where patients are less thin on the ground and cattle far greater. The North Eastern Honeydon, Grafton, Deddington, Scalded Blunham and Chippenham Village Trusts? No, none of these. Here is our HQ, The Long Yelling Trust, The Eyeworth Lodge, the Deadman and Holy Cross Trust, the Bury and Man's End! And why? Because I have filled the posts with nominees, who will, for a small charge, vacate their posts sideways like snakes to allow us to enter in.

STAN: Fuckin' sublime.

LIZZY: Outta this world!

BILLY: Common sense really - there is no regular register of employees or check ups, only ours. So welcome, you're all top execs, in place as soon as you fart, respected, decent and properly paid, far enough apart for no cross checks. And Pissy, beauty aids laid on as expenses! I will be Chief Regional Exec with my HQ at Man's End! There is no appeal against my decisions, and I can never resign until death do me part! *(ALL applaud. Sound of police sirens, shouts get closer)*

STAN :   Christ the men with the blue biros, black files, reports and placards, the slimy whistleblowers, are approaching fast. Time to scarper.

(ALL make to move off. STAN Stops, looks at audience)

STAN: Don't you think we should introduce ourselves before we go? After all they gave up their lunch for us - a greater sacrifice no man hath... or something..

BILLY: Outstanding, Stan. *(To audience)* 'Stan.' Put in another 'a', you know where, and you have his moniker and his true colours. Put a 'bub' at the end of mine and you have a fine leader of the pack. Look at Pissy Lizzy, just ask her where her home town is...?

STAN: Where's your home town, darling?

LIZZY: Bab-ill-on, baby!

BILLY   *(Caressing her body)*: The original Great One from there!

LIZZY: 'No Resuscitation!'

ALL: 'No resuscitation!'

LIZZY: 'Nil by mouth!'

ALL: 'Nil by mouth!'

BILLY: Give her a big hand, she's not joking!

                          (ALL applaud LIZZY. Face audience like a chorus line)

                          Well, who in the hell are we really?

ALL: We are the walkers of the Night,

                          Nothing less and nothing more,

                          We have left our claw-marks on your door,

                          And blood-stains cover every floor,

                          That and nothing more.

(ALL make clawing motions at audience)

BILLY: Onwards, fellow fiends, and (to AUDIENCE) we'll soon be back for more!

(Noises off; CROWD approaches, noises up, LIZZY, STAN, BILLY stroll, dance off. CUT LIGHTS. Faint lights up at back. Figure comes forward, FLORENCE NIGHTINGALE, in Victorian costume, as in the famous photo, holding her lamp. She raises it up over audience, pauses and whispers, 'Help, Help... CUT LIGHTS, EXIT FLORENCE. Echo of 'Help, help, help...' fades slowly into the Death March, five second snatch. CUT LIGHTS, SOUND. Pause as audience are on the way to the exits. Then up strongly Schubert's 'Trout Quartet,' piano section. Hold until auditorium is empty)

CURTAIN

THE PLAGUE

A fifteen-minute play

By

DEDWYDD JONES

<u>Performed at the Royal Court Theatre, London, July 2013,
directed by Vicky Featherstone</u>

(Living room; centre stage two chairs, MYFANWY, GARETH, sit waiting; thirties; cot, side stage, inside cot, babies (dolls!) in shawls)

MYFANWY: I tell you, Gareth, my womb is my own. They are invading my inner privacy! Stripping me of progeny! - band waggoners, gravy trainers, profiteers, skin grafters! Casting aside all idea of reasonable profit and hogging the lot! - down with all organs of local government, I say!

VOICE OF TOWN CRIER *(OFF STAGE):* Oyez! Oyez! Bring out your dead!

MYFANWY: See! Them and their stupid old plague! I bet they started it! But it's us who has to pay.

VOICE OF TOWN CRIER *(OFF STAGE):* Oyez, oyez. Bring out your dead!

MYFANWY: *(to GARETH)* Go on then!

(GARETH rushes to cot, lifts up 'baby' (a doll!) out of cot, rocks it gently, then hurls it into wings. Baby cries. Cut sound)

MYFANWY: Gareth! Show some respect!

GARETH: Sorry Myfanwy, wasn't thinking.

MYFANWY: Nearly all taken from us now.

GARETH: If only we'd had some warning.

MYFANWY: It's the Health Ministry…

GARETH: …now, dear, don't get morbid.

MYFANWY: Skin a flea for a penny they would, and skins don't come cheap, however tiny, they're selling them off in droves. I tell you, there isn't a God!

GARETH: *(Points upward)* Ssh! Not so loud.

VOICE OF TOWN CRIER *(OFF STAGE):* Oyez, oyez! Bring out your dead!

(GARETH takes up 'baby' from cot, carries it soothingly off stage. Sound of baby crying, cut sound. GARETH RE-ENTERS, with washing hands gestures)

MYFANWY: I love it when you're gentle with the refugees, Gareth, never mind if they are just cast- offs from alien hospices, even they are as sacred as we.

GARETH: There's a tender Mum you are too, my Myfanwy, you should get 'Carer' support instantly!

MYFANWY: *(Of cot)* How many left now?

GARETH: Three or four, give one or two, I'd say.

MYFANWY: Are they still breathing?

GARETH: Just.

MYFANWY: Scraping the barrel?

GARETH: Looks like.

MYFANWY: We've fulfilled our quota of little bodies! And 'More, more!' the damned Etonians demand, morning, noon and dinner time! Just greed now, bureaucratic greed, holding us to ransom. More, more, more, is their only song! *(Looking upward)* You up there, why are you torturing us like this? You and your pissing plague. Your fault! And plague of what, is what I ask? Nothing up there if you ask me, Gareth, just radio waves, that's all, just going to stupid NASA in Florida, yes, every one of them. Bloody Yanks.

GARETH: Ssh, love

MYFANWY: We're all just fleas on the world's back.

GARETH: That's better. Listen, like, we could still have more.

MYFANWY: What? At our time of death?

GARETH: Stand up. Walk the walk. *(MYFANWY walks like a sexy model)*

GARETH: Hey, Myfanwy, that dress, I mean, bloody gorgeous, like, it shows the line of your panties.

MYFANWY: Leave my panties out of this, we're in mourning.

GARETH: *(Gropes her)* To have more, we need less, of them, panties, I mean.

MYFANWY: Hands off! You've always treated our marriage like a dirty novel, haven't you?

GARETH: Page eighty-eight, heck, you and your 'b-u-m' *(Sings)* '...all in a heat wave.'

MYFANWY: You and your bloody dirty Freud!

GARETH: Freud's wife never had a moment of frigidity.

MYFANWY: And he never had a moment of rigidity...

GARETH: *(aside, to audience)* A quick parabasis... a chat aside, like the Greeks did, listen...

MYFANWY: ...Gareth, this is not the place... *(Of audience)* ... 'gentility' is their second name.

GARETH: Well, I am not to blame. Bend over.

MYFANWY: Why?

GARETH: For a quick f...f...f... ... fry up! I love you.

MYFANWY: My b.t.m. only...

GARETH: ...no, no...

MYFANWY: ...thou foul hound!

VOICE OFF TOWN CRIER *(OFF STAGE)*: Bring out your dead!

MYFANWY: Not again!

VOICE OF TOWN CRIER *(OFF STAGE)*: Oyez!

MYFANWY: Shut your gob!

VOICE OF TOWN CRIER: Bring out your…!

MYFANWY: …why? Why? Why?

GARETH: The plague thing, thing, thing!

MYFANWY: …what is it bloody then?

GARETH: Yes, you might flaming well ask!

MYFANWY: I think we ought to be told, I've said so a thousand times. *(Nods at cot)* Get a move on now , Gareth!

GARETH: *(GARETH Grabs doll (baby)drop-kicks it into audience)* Drop kick me, Jesu, through the goal posts of life!

VOICE OF TOWN CRIER: Oyez, oyez…

MYFANWY: ….oh, no, no, no! Down with your corpses! Bugger your plague pits, you greedy sodomites, good looking corpses mean nothing to you! The fairest maiden epiglottis in the world is wasted on you lot! Huh! *(Of cot)* Any left at all now?

GARETH: *(Glances in cot)* Not a sausage.

MYFANWY: Not one?

GARETH: All gone.

MYFANWY: What are we going to do?

GARETH: We mustn't dwell on anything. Look at it like the pragmatists of old Epidaurus. No more bottles, vitamins, teats, nappies – but lots of baby piggy-bank savings under the bed, coin, coin, coin!

MYFANWY: I never thought of it that way, Gareth, how keen you are.

GARETH: And the left-over charity garments..?

MYFANWY: ...they'll have to be sold right back to where they came from, situation must be faced. But now, in a global sense, Gareth, what is there left?

GARETH: Rooms, just empty rooms. In fact, six empty rooms.

MYFANWY: Yes...six empty cots.

GARETH: Six empty single cots

MYFANWY: That's a lot of empty single beds, six I mean.

GARETH: Six could be, no, now listen, love, six... little lodgers...

MYFANWY: ...shut your gob!

GARETH: **Paying** lodgers.

MYFANWY: You're a brute!

GARETH: Six is a lot of single **occupied** cots.

MYFANWY: Have you no feelings at all?

GARETH: At three seventy-five pence per diem, that makes…

MYFANWY: … don't go on! I mean, just slowly. But…these numbers, got to face up to them, whatever the casualties.

GARETH: Times are short, Myfanwy.

MYFANWY: Got to be realistic.

GARETH: Even if we had 450 solid gold watches by Versace, we would still need more.

MYFANWY: 'More, more and still more' is a reasonable song when sung by us!

GARETH: *(To audience)* I feel like a parabasis again, bless the old Greeks. All I got to say is I love Myfanwy, I can't help it, I love her day and nighties, I love her pant and panties! I'll love her till kingdom come, all on account of her glorious bum!

MYFANWY: *(Aside)* Bleeedin' arsehole! To think I sold our rose and carnation three-piece suite for him! Hey, over to me now, mate!

GARETH: *(To audience)* Nice little chat, eh, people? But Lady calls. Myfanwy, I believe a whole new life is opening up for us.

VOICE OF TOWN CRIER (OFF STAGE): Oyez, oyez! Bring out your dead!

MYFANWY: Jesus! They're sucking us dry. And think of the price of skin, even old ones! *(Dog barks off stage)* Did you hear that?

GARETH: *(calls to dog)* Yes. Rover, boy! Here, good boy, here. Good boy. *(Mimes stroking dog)*

MYFANWY: *(To audience)* Dear old family retainer. So human!

MYFANWY, GARETH: *(together, caressing ROVER)* Rover! Rover! Rover! Woof, woof, woof!

GARETH: Myfanwy, stop! Sorry, he'll have to go.

MYFANWY: This imbecilic plague! Just an excuse for official expenses, and it's us who pays in the end, the ordinary Mum in the street. But you're right again, no kids for our lovely old Rover to play with.

GARETH: And he's a big eater.

(EXIT GARETH, sound of a shot. GARETH RE-ENTERS carrying dead dog)

GARETH: *(Makes sign of cross over dog)* God bless you, old Rover, boyo. *(HURLS DEAD DOG off stage.*
GARETH   *EXITS after dog. MYFANWY waves dog goodbye. GARETH re-enters, with letters, leaflets)* And look at what I found in the letter box. Usual ads for chicken tikas and onion bhajies. And this. Brown

envelopes I do not love. 'Department of Health…'

MYFANWY: …bloody Shylocks, pounds of flesh is all they think of.

GARETH: *(Reads)* It's more information about the Plague, yes, "…terminal stages are marked by strange and violent self-strangulations…" Look, the pic here. Like this*! (GARETH strangles himself to floor, MYFANWY follows suit, they get up, gasping)*

MYFANWY: But what is this bloody Plague?

GARETH: '…a plague of …it says here *(Reads)* of 'Ava…' Aver…' 'Aver…' 'ryce'?

MYFNWY: Curry recipe, is it?

GARETH: Aver…rice.

MYFANWY: All bloody horse-meat now. Such a shame.

GARETH: Bark like a dog, neigh like a horse, it's all one in the bin!

MYFANWY: Tell me what's going on, Gareth.

GARETH: 'Avarice.'

MYFANWY: What's that?

GARETH: Greed, greed is busting out all over!

MYFANWY: But we are as innocent as babes in a cot.

GARETH: We must learn to go naked.

MYFANWY: You got no trouble with that.

GARETH: Listen, they know it, we know it - well-formed new-born Caucasian infants are worth their weight in solid Swiss francs, pelf ineffable, to say the least. Bend over.

MYFANWY: This is no baby farm. This is no Eden and I'm no Eve.

GARETH: My love, it is now a matter of simple survival for us.

MYFANWY: We breed them, we feed them, they cream us.

GARETH: *(Begins to caress her)* You could even sell your eggs.

MYFANWY: That is one thing I would never do.

(GARETH caresses)

GARETH: Why not, love?

MYFANWY: Because they are duck eggs!

GARETH: *(Stops caressing)* Well, well, well...

MYFANWY: ...the Market...

GARETH: …listen, we'd better get on with it, fill the cot again, throw in a few tiny Taffs for free, and cash-money this time. No plastic. No skin off our noses.

GARETH: Great idea! Look for the silver lining.

MYFANWY: Perhaps there is a God after all.

GARETH: I've always said so, haven't I?

MYFANWY: But our cot is empty.

GARETH: Not for long. With our baby-farm Eden rising to heights of productivity, we'll soon be a part of the great economic revival. Bless our glorious Exchequer and his libido! It's a long time coming, and it's not far off…

(GARETH mimes shagging MYFANWY. Grunts and groans)

MYFANWY: Don't stop! Don't stop!

VOICE OF TOWN CRIER *(OFF STAGE):* Oyez! Bring out your dead!

MYFANWY: *(EMBRACING GARETH)* Don't stop, don't stop…

VOICE OF TOWN CRIER *(OFF STAGE):* Oyez! Bring out your dead!

GARETH: *(Shouts over his shoulder)* Bloody 'ell…!… give us a chance, will you, you bloody pen-pushers!

(They shag frantically for a few seconds)

(CUT LIGHTS. EXIT GARETH, MYFANWY. ENTER CLERGYMAN, dog collar, pious, smiling sweetly, looks into audience, clasps hands)

CLERGYMAN: Hello there. Thank you all so much for coming along this lovely evening, when you could be in that nice pub on the corner. *(Gestures to stage)* What we're asking now, isn't it, is - what part does the Church play in all this? Yes, yes..? *(Benignly, making sign of cross over cot, then audience)* God bless you, my children.

(EXIT CLERGYMAN. CUT LIGHTS)

VOICE OF TOWN CRIER *(OFF STAGE, FADING):* Oyez....Oyez...

CURTAIN

Titles from Creative Print Publishing Ltd

Fiction

The Shadow Line & The Secret Sharer
ISBN 978-0-9568535-0-9

Joseph Conrad

Kristina's Destiny
ISBN 978-0-9568535-1-6

Diana Daneri

Andrew's Destiny
ISBN 978-0-9568535-2-3

Diana Daneri

To Hold A Storm
ISBN 978-0-9568535-3-0

Chris Green

Ten Best Short Stories of 2011
ISBN 978-0-9568535-5-4

Various

The Lincoln Letter
ISBN 978-0-9568535-4-7

Gretchen Elhassani

Dying to Live
ISBN 978-0-9568535-7-8

Katie L. Thompson

Keeping Karma
ISBN 978-0-9568535-6-1

Louise Reid

Escape to the Country
ISBN 978-0-9568535-8-5

Patsy Collins

Lindsey's Destiny
ISBN 978-0-9568535-9-2

Diana Daneri

ANGELS UNAWARES
ISBN 978-1-909049-02-4

Dedwydd Jones

RELICK
ISBN 978-1-909049-03-1

Steven Gepp

It Hides In Darkness
ISBN 978-1-909049-04-8

Ross C. Hamilton

Transmission of Evil
ISBN 978-1-909049-06-2

Mandy Sheering

Ransom
ISBN 978-1-909049-07-9

Don Nixon

Milwaukee Deep
ISBN 978-1-909049-05-5

G. Michael

PANDORA
ISBN 978-1-909049-09-3

Marcus Woolcott

Alaric, Child Of The Goths
ISBN 978-1-909049-08-6

Daniel F. Bowman

For Catherine
ISBN 978-1-909049-01-7

Elizabeth Morgan

Black Book on the Welsh Theatre
ISBN 978-1-909049-11-6

Dedwydd Jones

MASKS or The Golden Omega
ISBN 978-1-909049-13-0

Dedwydd Jones

The Lazis Project
ISBN 978-1-909049-14-7

Marcus Woolcott

NonFiction

Amazonia – My Journey Into The Unknown
ISBN 978-1-909049-00-0

Adam Wikierski

Recollections of Pathos and the Greek Islands
ISBN 978-1-909049-12-3

Les Burgess

Contacting Creative Print Publishing Ltd

Creative Print Publishing are publishers of books covering various genres including all kinds of fiction, non-fiction and life histories.

For more details contact:

Creative Print Publishing Ltd
Creative Print Studios
Rear of No 7, Broomfield Road
Marsh
Huddersfield
HD1 4QD

United Kingdom

Web: http://www.creativeprintpublishing.com

Email: info@creativeprintpublishing.com Tel:

+44 (0) 1484 314 985